D0938320

BRO

ALSO BY ROBERT NEWTON PECK

A Day No Pigs Would Die

A Part of the Sky

Soup (a series)

Nine Man Tree

Cowboy Ghost

Extra Innings

Horse Thief

BRO

A NOVEL

ROBERT NEWTON PECK

HARPERCOLLINS*PUBLISHERS*

Bro

 Printed in the United States of America. For information address HarperCollins Children's Books, a division of HarperCollins Publishers, 1350 Avenue of the Americas, New York, NY 10019.

www.harperchildrens.com

Library of Congress Cataloging-in-Publication Data
Peck, Robert Newton.
Bro / by Robert Newton Peck.—1st ed.
p. cm.
Summary: Young Tug Dockery witnesses a brutal act by his grandfather that leaves him unable to speak, so when his parents die, Tug's beloved older brother feels compelled to escape from a hellish labor camp to rescue him from their grandfather's Florida cattle ranch.
ISBN 0-06-052974-1 — ISBN 0-06-052975-X (lib. bdg.)
[1. Brothers—Fiction. 2. Mutism, Elective—Fiction.
3. Grandfathers—Fiction. 4. Florida—History—
20th Century—Fiction.] I. Title.
PZ7.P339Br 2004 2003056648
[Fic]—dc22 CIP
AC

Typography by Andrea Vandergrift
1 2 3 4 5 6 7 8 9 10

First Edition

With fervent gratitude, Bro *is dedicated to:*
My wife. Sam typed it.
Michele Redmond, who knows horses.
The Mazak family of Mabel, Florida . . .
who are really and truly cattle crackers.
Kathleen and Andy Burleson.
Nancy and Rock Spearman.
Jan and Buddy Williams of Manchester, Georgia.
Calvary, Georgia . . . and her Mule Day.
Each and every donkey in the world.
Best of all . . . to mules. *May these willing animals*
be given the tender care they deserve.

Robert Newton Peck
Longwood, Florida

DOCKERY

Family Tree

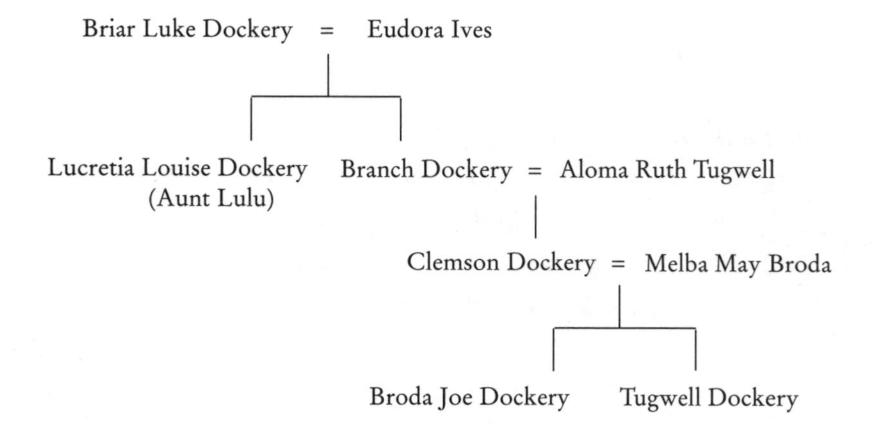

BRO

PROLOGUE

Florida: 1933

A giant hissing snake of steel and steam.

Half a mile in length, the black serpent began to slither forward, spurred by the engineer's oily glove on her throttle.

A chain of couplings snapped into contact with a series of metallic clanks. Gradually, the great locomotive lurched forward, gaining ground, increasing her speed. Above the arrowhead prow, her cyclops eye pierced the inky darkness with a lance of light. The wheels of forty-four freight cars, each weighing more than one hundred tons, turned faster and faster. The charging train became a curving bullwhip of iron and power, able to demolish anything and anyone in her path.

With a lower arm resting upon the sill of the

cabin's open window, the engineer wiped moisture from his goggles. Leaving them off, he squinted ahead into a billowing mist. The chilly night forced him to turn up his jacket's collar. Although thirsting for another swallow of hot coffee from his thermos, he refrained, concentrating on track visibility.

What little there was of it. . . .

Fifty miles to the south, on a deserted and unlit rural road, a dented, rusty Ford sedan was heading for the tiny Florida town of Yazoo City. Busy windshield wipers were wagging, clicking left and right, fighting the fog. Alone on the backseat, curled beneath a worn and scratchy U.S. Army blanket of olive drab, a nine-year-old boy tried to sleep. But could not.

Fists tightening, Tugwell Dockery remembered the last time he'd been taken to visit his grandparents. At age three. The horrid and haunting memory had become a painful scar.

On the front seat, his parents, Clemson and Melba May Dockery, were bickering, like usual. More than once, his daddy tipped up a bottle inside a brown paper bag, twisted at the neck.

Tug heard him cuss a sorry word.

"Do have another dumb drink," the wife taunted him, her voice raking the night. "Admit that you're lost."

"Ain't. Taking a shortcut. Ahead of us there used to was a grade crossing that humps up and over a railroad track. Pebble road. Nobody use it much."

"This trip's already a waste. Not to mention boring. Car radio's been on the blink for most a year," she whined. "But *you'll* never get it replaced."

"Oh, hush up. The doggone *clutch* is what needs repairing. Slips so bad, it's a miracle to shift gears. But why pour money we don't got into a machine we owe payments on?"

She sighed. "We should've stayed in Georgia. Instead we have to sneak back to Yazoo, like foreigners, where everybody stares at us as though we're diseased."

"It's my pa's birthday."

With a grunt, she said, "Branch is too over-the-hill to know it. A lot you care. We haven't bothered with his birthday for years. You probable plan to mooch him for another loan."

"I'll pay back."

"Ha! Maybe when you-know freezes."

"Melba May, we's in a depression. Times are tough. On my customer route, everyone's too busted broke to buy lightning rods or fire insurance. Boss plans to can me."

"Swell." She paused. "God's punishing us, Clem, for sins. That's the reason Broda Joe went wrong and got sent to *prison*." She whispered the word. "That's why we had to leave Yazoo and move to Georgia. Tugwell hasn't spoke a word since he was three. Not even prayers."

In the backseat, Tug was hearing it all again, biting his lower lip to make himself hurt, wanting to jump out of the Ford, leave his arguing parents forever, run away and find Bro. Trouble was, Broda Joe Dockery, now eighteen, had been a prisoner in a Florida labor camp for two years. Another year to go.

Tug hated living without Bro.

Now, his lonely life was fixing to worsen. Soon as they arrived in Yazoo, he'd have to face Grampap, Branch Joseph Dockery, a mean old white-haired coot. He'd done terrible things that day when Tug was only three.

In his mind, Tugwell kept seeing it happen, over and over, hearing his grandfather's rage, and then the brutality and the blood. Watching, his mouth had opened into a silent scream. For six years, Tugwell Dockery had not spoken a word. All he could do was see, hear, think—and remember, remember, remember.

Only his brother understood.

"Ah! There it be, Melba May."

His father's sudden remark opened Tug's eyes; but beneath the blanket, there was nothing to look at. Nothing to hear except the tires grinding the gravel.

"Up there?" Melba May asked, alarmed.

"Yup. If'n she'll make it. Up and over that there grade crossing, just as I told you, and we'll be coasting into Yazoo by the back way. Here we go."

"Not now! I hear a train, Clemson. So tarry until it passes by." She slapped his shoulder. "Whenever you guzzle likker, you drive like a lunatic."

Eyes open, feeling the ground tremble under their car, Tug was aware that a strong light was penetrating the dirty windows and growing brighter. A rumbling grew louder as his father tried to gun the motor. His mother cried out. But a train whistle, shrieking as though in panic, muffled her scream.

His father swore. "Damn the cussed clutch."

"Clem, we're on the tracks!"

"I can make it."

Those were Clemson Dockery's last words. The locomotive smashed the front door of their car. Sparks spewed as metal scraped metal, blending with the noise of crushing steel and shattering glass. The collapsed car rolled and tumbled, finally bouncing off the rails, to lie in a mangled heap of gnawed wreckage. Freight car after freight car roared through the dust and fumes of spilled gasoline.

Most of the Ford burst into flame.

It took two miles for the locomotive to brake to a complete stop. An hour later, after a cautious reversing and swinging of lanterns, neither the shaken engineer nor his coal-tender fireman could locate any human remains among the scattered, smoldering debris. Just bits of trash and a bent Georgia license plate, which they eventually surrendered to a uniformed deputy. They were about to abandon searching when they spotted a young boy. Trembling, he stood thirty feet from the train tracks, mouth open and head bleeding, clutching an army blanket.

When questioned, the child tried to speak. Yet said nothing. Crouching, with a knee to the ground, the boy's unsteady fingertip drew three distinct letters in the damp Florida sand.

CHAPTER 1

Not quite noon.

Percival Sweetbutter, the chief of police in Yazoo City, Florida, held a bent and battered Georgia license plate in one hammy hand, a telephone in the other.

Percy leaned back in the swivel desk chair, his two hundred and sixty pounds twanging the springs like a plucked banjo. He hooked the heel of a hefty cowboy boot on the lower open drawer.

With a slow smile, he said, "Farley, thank you. That's nifty news. The boy is still frighted, naturally, but no serious injury? Soon as Doc Munson's got him patched into prosperity, do bring him around, so's we can determine where he rightful belong. And cheer him some."

Percy listened as the deputy reported how the young survivor didn't hanker to answer any questions.

"He's probable in shock. The poor little shaver took one whale of a wallop." Percy's smile broadened. "A ice cream cone ought to ease his spirits. See ya both sudden."

Twenty minutes later, two adjacent soda-fountain stools were occupied at The Candy Kitchen—one by a bandaged boy, another by a six-and-a-half-foot peace officer. The chief read a flavor list from the wall that faced them, above a long mirror: "Chocolate, vanilla, black raspberry, coffee, maple walnut, cherry, peach, butter pecan, and my favorite . . . strawberry." He eyed his silent guest. "Okay by you if'n I order one for each of us?" He laughed. "But certain not one of each for each of us."

As though in a trance, the child nodded.

During his first lick of strawberry, the chief reviewed his early-morning communication with the Georgia Bureau of Motor Vehicles. The demolished car had been registered to a Mr. Clemson Dockery of Moultrie, Georgia. Nobody to home when he called. He then phoned the only Dockery listed in Yazoo City, an ornery old rancher who resided miles out of town, whom he'd met once or twice. Impossible to know everyone in the county on a first-name basis. He suspected there was a Dockery family that moved to Georgia. Without their elder son.

"Mr. Branch Dockery? This is Chief Sweetbutter."

An elderly voice about spat. "Is this about more trouble that dang Broda Joe's mixed into? The young whelp is already behind bars."

Percy paused. "Yes, we have noticed a Broda Joe Dockery on our Pecan County prison roster. He your son?"

"Grandson."

Percy shook his head. "Would he happen to have a kid brother, about the age of eight or nine?"

"Reckon. Ain't seen Tugwell since he was maybe three." A pause. "Why you calling me?"

The rancher listened to Percy's full account of a car being bashed by a freight train and an injured child. The raspy old voice said, "I ain't fit to tend a youngster. However, I'll call my sister, Lucretia." With no further comment, he hung up.

Odd, Percy thought. Stone cold.

While at The Candy Kitchen, he also ordered a cup of coffee and, for the child, a banana and a chocolate doughnut with colored sprinkles. Both were eaten without comment.

"Tugwell, I'd imagine you might git called Tug for short. Does your grandfather call you Tug sometimes? Bet he do."

No response. As though he had questioned a fence post. With a paper napkin, Percy gently wiped a spot of chocolate from a corner of the lad's mouth.

Beside him sat a mite of mystery.

CHAPTER 2

You don't understand.

I had me a notion to tell Chief Sweetbutter about the train last night, and how awful sorry it hurt, burning up my mother and daddy. It bothered me that I couldn't feel more sadness. Like I was numb all over. Didn't actual care.

"A jailbird and a dumbo," my father had said about Bro and me—more than once—and Mama didn't disagree. The kids in Georgia called me a dumbo, too, because of my silence. Thought me deaf, and stupid. They made me hate school.

I knew different.

Inside my brain I talked all the time, and proper words got spoken. Yet I wasn't ready to sound them out or force them off my tongue. Broda Joe knew. We were brothers. Always and forever. He wasn't bad like everyone said.

Looking up at the chief, my mind was saying: *Thanks for the eats, sir. I'm truly beholden. Honest I am.*

To prove it, I allowed the police chief to rest a paw on my shoulder as we crossed the street. Weren't many cars, so I figured that the chief was trying to supply friendship as well as protection.

As we returned to the Yazoo police station, a black Model T was arriving in one powerful hurry. Out hopped a woman I guessed to be a hundred years old, bolting from the car like a rooster after a June bug. Despite her puny size, she spoke right up as though she owned all of Florida.

"Officer, I am Miss Lucretia Louise Dockery. I heard some dreadful news on the radio, down to Rickapee, where I reside. Then my brother phoned. Had to jump in my car and break every speed law to reach here."

Aunt Lulu!

She didn't get along with my parents, so I guess that's why she'd always avoided us. However, I'd met her a couple of times before we moved to Georgia. She was sort of a hermit. Bro always talked about her, liked her a lot. My brother claimed everyone in Pecan County was cautious of her, including gators, boar hogs, and sharks. Must be the truth, because one glance made Chief Percival Sweetbutter remove his cowboy hat and give her a respectful bow.

"How do, Miss Dockery. I been in touch with a Mr. Branch Dockery and— "

"Branch is my kid brother. He's only seventy. We're two years apart but not near enough miles. That man is so cantankerous he'd piddle on a petunia." She pointed at me. "Is this who I believe?"

The chief nodded. "Yes'm. Presume so. From all reports, this here youngster be Tugwell Dockery from up Georgia way. We've already identified their license plate. However, he is— "

"Save it." Aunt Lulu held up a halting hand, palm forward. "I've come to take full responsibility for him."

"Well now, according to law, Miss Dockery, and seeing that his parents are deceased and his brother is serving correctional time, the grandfather is legally next of kin, and thereby officially— "

"Ha! You can kiss my *un*official foot." She stomped her shoe. "Branch isn't fit to be put in charge of a dead rat. I trucked myself to the Pecan

County prison, twice, to visit and console Broda Joe, this child's brother. He gave me a earful about Branch. That crusty old geezer hasn't been to see his grandson even a once." She raised a finger. "Not one time."

Took me only a breath to realize Aunt Lucretia was fond of Bro, even though nobody else in our family seemed to be.

Bro! I want to find Bro. There was no way to tell these people. *Bro and I don't have to talk. He understands. Because he was there when it happened, on the day my grandfather went crazy mad.*

My brother figured I'd seen it all. Later on, he throwed a rock through the schoolhouse window and shook his fist at the open-mouth teachers. The ones that claimed they couldn't learn somebody who never talked.

I was six.

Broda Joe was fifteen.

That's about when Bro quit school to transport likker. And got caught. My parents wouldn't hire him a lawyer. They told me that Broda Joe was a disgrace. A criminal. I couldn't tell them the truth. But I knew it inside my heart.

Bro was good clean through.

CHAPTER 3

Aunt Lulu gunned the engine.

"First stop," she told me, "will be the Baptist church."

Seeing me flinch, she hurriedly explained that we were seeking neither prayer nor salvation, but something far more needful. Clothes. Due to the accident, I was inside all of the duds I had with me.

Add to that, she said the Baptist secondhand clothes were clean and free. Seeing as I was dusted with dirt and hadn't a penny to my person, *free* was an okay price. I'd had no new clothes in a while. When Bro got shipped to jail, my mother dunked herself into religion, like Daddy into whiskey; so Aunt Lulu's practical nature got us off on the right foot.

"Know in advance," Aunt Lulu said later as we went motoring past the Fat Chef Diner and out of Yazoo, "in many a way, I want you to grow up to favor Broda Joe. That boy has more guts, gumption, and backbone than a few who scowl at him, and sour his name."

The Model T turned off the county highway, which was paved with blacktop, and onto a gravel road that seemed to point nowhere.

"Worry not," she informed me. "I know where we're going. Branch and I were hatched and raised on this ranch, over seventy years ago. The place and the beef cattle are half his, half mine. Decades ago, when Branch got hitched to Aloma Ruth Tugwell, I moved out and went to live and work part-time as a bookkeeper in nearby Rickapee. We two were like sisters. Fine woman, Aloma, but a mite frail. Nothing like Branch, who was always stouter than oak. He was leather while she was lace. But I packed up and left as a courtesy. My remaining would've been the third wheel on a buckboard."

One of the car's front tires hit a deep pothole and shook both of us to a rattle. Great-aunt Lucretia spat out a swear word that I didn't imagine ladies used. A real zinger.

"Pardon," she said.

I sort of flashed her a thumbs-up shrug.

"Our vocabulary may have its shortcomings," Aunt Lulu said, "but there's nothing wrong with our eardrums. Yours or mine."

With a grin, I let her know she was on target. Both of my ears worked like a watchdog's and I even sang silent songs. On key. Thinking about music usual made me feel joyous. It almost did now. But when the Model T scooted between a pair of high wooden posts and under an arch that boasted a twig-constructed cattle brand, my face fell to a frown. It stood for the Diamond Dee, and naturally meant it was Dockery prime land.

Aunt Lulu patted my left kneecap. "Now don't you worry, lamb. I know a sorry event took place here six years ago, one that you were witness to. Aloma Ruth's death. But my brother was once a decent gentleman. Prior to the tragedy, Bro admired his grampap." She sighed. "Memories. I was here when Branch first slapped Bro's young rump atop a horse."

Hearing the word *horse* gave me the sudden all-over chills. When I was three I'd seen the horses die. Four of them. Nothing could wipe out this awful memory from my mind.

No! I shouted. *Turn around*, I was trying to say. *If you don't, I'll jump out of your car and run away. Somehow I can locate Bro so we can be brothers again.*

Aunt Lulu couldn't hear my yelling. Nobody could, except for Broda Joe, but he was locked up at a labor camp, somewhere here in Pecan County, Florida.

Stop. Maybe I ought to go back to Georgia. Saying it to myself woke me with a jolt, to realize there wouldn't be anybody there. Mother and Daddy were now yelling at each other in Heaven, or somewhere warmer, and my brother was serving time. How could I get my brain to quit hollering *Stop Stop Stop*?

What I ached for was to have Bro and me scamper away together. We both ought to escape bad places. Yet wishing for it was just a pipe dream.

Forcing myself to look through the car window, I saw small bunches of cows on my right, each group crowding a syrup tank to lick molasses off a spin wheel for fattening. A lot of cows, yet no horses. Not a one. Ahead loomed a two-story whitewashed house with a typical Florida tin roof. Shingles slanted over the front porch. As we neared, I noticed several missing fence rails. Others broken. A shutter hung crooked and downhearted.

The place had no pride.

Aunt Lulu braked to a whoa and tooted the horn a blaring blast. "Let's dump ourselfs out, Tugwell. Your grandfather's always here, on account he's got nowhere to go, and nobody to call a friend."

A moment later, a lame old person shuffled around a house corner, coming from a gray barn of unpainted pine. He looked bent and broken, as if bad luck had wiped its boots on him. Or kicked him until it hurt to walk. He was no longer the sturdy Branch Dockery I recalled.

But I still hated his guts.

CHAPTER 4

Branch recognized his sister's car.

She came every six weeks or so to check on her half of the ranch. And to boss him. The old biddy was seventy-two. Why in Hades couldn't she just die and quit pestering? Earlier, there was the telephone call from Chief Sweetbutter; now he had to contend with Lucretia Louise. She hadn't come alone. There was a child at her side, a boy in bandages, with eyes that judged him.

Tugwell.

Just seeing the boy, Branch felt shame encircle his neck as a hang rope, choking off breathing and causing his heart to palpitate. Tugwell didn't look at him, but through him, as though Branch Dockery was made of breakable glass. Brittle.

Aware he had stopped, Branch forced himself to continue toward the car.

"Lucretia," he grunted.

"Branch," she responded. "I brung you a somebody you've not seen in a spell. Your second grandchild, who bears the proud name of Tugwell."

Branch froze, unable to budge.

"Tug," his sister said, "you best extend your right hand in a manly fashion, to greet your grandfather."

Forcing himself, Branch took Tug's outstretched hand. Although the fingers were young and small, he sensed a surprising strength, a firmness he hadn't anticipated. "Welcome," was all he could say, presuming that Lucretia Louise, as usual, would tote a pack load of palaver.

"He is nine," she announced.

Nine. Branch recalled when Broda Joe was nine. Bro's kid brother had a similar look. A strong jaw.

"Mules," he said. "I work mules now."

It sounded clumsy. Lame. He hoped this lad could understand without more explaining. Never again would there be horses on the Diamond

Dee, as he couldn't suffer the sight of them. A memory that continued to grind him into grist.

Lucretia and Tugwell were studying him as though he was a freak. Why didn't they go away?

"Come around," Branch told his sister and grandchild. "My mules are by the barn." As they walked, he added, "Their names are Theodore and Maude. He's a mule and she's a hinny." Resting a boot on the bottom rail of the corral fence, Branch waited for the mules to come. They did, and he caressed their soft muzzles. "Good workers. Both Maude and Theo got sound cattle sense. More'n I got."

Lucretia Louise nodded.

CHAPTER 5

O'Grady sorted the mail hisself.

He'd done so for eleven years, ever since his promotion from head guard up to superintendent of the Pecan County Correctional Labor Camp. Being a warden was a catbird seat job.

Every week or about, some cluck of a relative mailed a bill or two of cash to one of the thirty-nine prisoners. O'Grady could usual tell by the look or feel if a envelope contain money. If'n so, the letter got tore up and throwed away. The dough found his pocket.

Same with goody packages.

His piggy eyes always widen whenever comic books got sent. Even though they wasn't easy to read. Was also Hershey's bars, cookies, apples, fresh bread, and doughnuts. Little of it reached prisoners. Instead, it went directly to Ogre O'Grady's waistline. He now weighted over three hundred pound, and still prospering.

Year ago, one a the jailbirds got wise.

Calbin Smithfielder, a ass-ache prisoner, claim he wunt receiving what his folks send. Recalling the incident, Ogre chuckled. Ain't it dreadful that Smithfielder took a bullet while, as the saying go, attempting to escape. Only gut shot. Mere wounding a bird didn't git reported. Be a shame to kill Smithfielder and stop all them packages.

No bird had ever fly away during Ogre's eleven years as Boss Man. A few dumbos try. Thirteen buried out yonder in the swamp. No one escape. At night, every con's ankle git shackled to the iron foot bar of his metal cot. If he run, he drag a cot with him. District director give him a certificate for his office wall. Framed. A perfect ten-year record. Felt swaggery to be thought of as a model civil servant.

Ogre could spot the trouble doers.

For certain, one them young Turks that bore extra watching was the Dockery kid: Broda Joe Dockery from Yazoo. The state troopers had collared him driving a decoy car. Likker. Moonlight farming. Only sixteen at the time. Dockery been in his custody two year. One more to go.

Judge give him three years hard.

Dockery's folks never sent him no letters. Not from neither his pa or his ma. Nary a word. Just visits from some auntie. A tough ol' hen. Few women would come to a labor camp full of convicts.

Cruel, the way young Dockery got treated by the older inmates . . . mainly Crit Zaggert, who called this boy Girlie Face. Ogre didn't care. The foul treatment serve to break a new convict's spirit. Shame him down into the dirt. The humiliation would grind Dockery to humble. And obedient.

Ogre distrust all of his campers. Some more'n others. This young Dockery snot got a uppity chin. Defiant. Sometimes he didn't snatch off his hat soon enough when spoke to. A few kicks from metal-toe boots had cured him of such. As a guard, Walter Patrick O'Grady had pride hisself as the toughest and meanest screw. Also the biggest. It earned him the nickname that he enjoy to git called . . . Ogre.

After he learnt what's it mean.

CHAPTER 6

It was dark.

Aunt Lulu had come prepared, and made up two upstairs beds. One for herself, and the other for me. Across the hall.

Good thing. On account I sure wasn't going to remain alone here all night with old Branch, even though I liked meeting Theodore and Maude. Aunt Lucretia never intended to dump me and leave. She told me so, and I decided to believe everything she said. Bro always claimed our great-aunt was as straight out as a left jab.

Aunt Lulu looked more tired than a worn rag.

Following our arrival at the Diamond Dee, she'd attacked the downstairs for hours with a broom and a mop, cleaning everything that didn't move. She washed a load of Branch's dirty clothes plus the few I had, scrubbed pots and pans, and took a swipe at the cobwebs. Then she cooked us a meal. Had ol' Branch dared to object, Aunt Lulu would've took a swipe at him.

"You," she told Branch at supper, "live like a tramp."

When I was final in bed, Aunt Lulu touched my freshly swabbed face the way you'd stroke the nose of a mule. She left me to stare at the ceiling, its cracks, and the peeling paint. That ol' Branch was hard to understand. Ate silent, then stomped upstairs without a word. His face as sour as bad weather.

Bro, if I knew where you's at, I'd clear out of here pronto and rescue you from the labor camp.

Outside on a oak limb, a owl was hooting. He sure made the whippoorwills turn quiet. A long way distant, a dog barked and then stilled. Clutching an edge of the sheet with both hands, I listened to the quacking of tree frogs. Like ducks.

Bro.

After what happened here on this awful ranch, when we still lived in Yazoo, my parents seemed annoyed that I couldn't talk. And stopped speaking to me. But Broda Joe would sneak into my room at night and tell me stuff.

As he talked, I'd listen.

"Tug, don't you worry about speaking. Ain't no big deal. Plenty of people talk but don't do it pleasant. Ma and Pa yap at each other constant. Remember last Sunday afternoon, at the baseball game? The fans yelling rotten at the umpire, Frank Foy, even though you couldn't find a feller finer than Frank."

To teach me letters and words, Bro borrowed picture books from the Yazoo City Free Library. Before I turn six, he had me reading, always questioning me to make certain I understood, and I'd nod if I did. That was our system.

"Tug, you're one smart little whipper. Keep talking to yourself. Quiet like, as though you're reading. Then, when you be alone, say a word out loud. Slow and easy. Don't never try to speak at a person, not even *me*, until you be ready. Catch on?"

I nodded.

"It'll come, Tug, but ya can't force it. Takes time. Before it's ready, not even Mother Nature can rip open a rosebud into a rose."

I final fell asleep that first night at the Diamond Dee thinking about my brother.

If a rose could open for anyone, it would be Bro.

CHAPTER 7

Percival Sweetbutter slowed his official Yazoo City vehicle along a stretch of ten-foot-high barbed razor-wire containment fence to stop at a chained security gate.

"Got bidness here, chief?" a surly guard asked. He was sloppy dressed and could use a shave. Probable a bath. His left hand was holding a scatter. Twelve gauge.

"If not," Percy answered, "I'd choose to be elsewhere."

"Captain O'Grady don't cotton to visitors."

"Open up, please. Or I'll have this junkyard inspected by state authorities, and you'll be seeking alternative employment." The gate was promptly unlocked and opened. With a polite touch to the brim of his cowboy hat, Percy said,

"Son, thanks for your courtesy," and drove through, hearing the heavy steel slam behind him as if annoyed.

The Pecan County Correctional Labor Camp was not a place that Chief Sweetbutter enjoyed visiting. To his left, four black men and three whites worked barefoot, stripped to the waist, backs shining with sweat, to hoist a fallen log from a mucky swale. The water was dark and muddy. Nearby, a uniformed rider sat a horse. A sawed-off shotgun lay crosswise behind the saddle horn.

'Twas a long working day for those poor devils. Perhaps without a midday meal.

Driving by the dog pens, he counted four bloodhounds. Three were lying on dirt, sleeping. The fourth was scratching his backside on a corner post. Percy wondered how often the bloodhounds were led to a empty bed inside the cement block structures to inhale the scent of a missing prisoner. Then, baying and barking, start their pursuit into the surrounding swamp, followed by men and weaponry. Unless a gator got the first bite. There were more'n a few giants floating in the black water. Some stretched to thirteen foot, all prehistoric teeth, jaws, and hunger.

The alligators offered the runaway a quick

death. A choice. Perhaps preferable to waiting for the hounds. And then a lashing.

Percy had brought a mug shot of Broda Joe, which he now compared to the three white men. Satisfied that Dockery was not among them, he concluded that he best check in with Ogre O'Grady. He located him, sucking on a toothpick, in a extra-large rocking chair, under shade. A colored prisoner in a zebra suit was buffing Ogre's boot.

Exiting his parked vehicle, Percy felt obliged to say "Good day."

"You lost?" the Boss Man replied.

"If'n I was, I'd sure dislike to be found here. Reason I come is to afford personal information to one a yourn."

"Who'd that be?"

"Name of Dockery, Broda J."

Ogre's piggy eyes narrowed. "Well, seems that skinny little Dockery ain't receiving guests today, on account he's occupy the cool box."

This metal cube was positioned in blazing heat and was anything but cool. Inside the box, a problem prisoner was close to roasted alive.

"Fetch him out."

O'Grady spat. "On whose orders?"

Percy had come prepared. Pulling a document

from a shirt pocket, he said, "Judge Hannah T. Singletary has obliged us with a court order, to inform your prisoner of a family death. All legal. For you to deny my seeing him would amount to a defiance of procedure, one that could terminate your comfy career . . . Captain."

In less than two minutes, a near-naked boy crawled from the hole, blinking in sun, his frail body awash by perspiration. He looked nothing like the photograph. Broda Joe Dockery appeared as a trapped and frightened animal. Percy identified welts on his shoulders and back. He was in sorry shape.

"Dockery?" Percy asked in disbelief. "Broda Joe Dockery?"

"Yes." The boy coughed. "Yessir."

Fortunately a water pump was nearby. Leading the feeble prisoner to it, Chief Sweetbutter primed and pumped the iron handle. Broda Joe drank and rinsed off like a crazed beast, while Percy glared at O'Grady with restrained contempt. A pity he couldn't right the unspeakable wrongs to this lad.

"Son," he said, "it is my duty to notify you with sorry news. Your parents, Mr. and Mrs. Clemson Dockery, was killt by a freight train striking their automobile."

The boy's face registered alarm.

"Tug? Oh God, please . . . not Tug."

"Tugwell Dockery survived. Your kid brother and I enjoyed some strawberry ice cream together. So don't worry. He got treated by Doctor Munson, and is sound and safe, in the care of Miss Lucretia Louise Dockery."

The prisoner cracked a weak smile. "Aunt Lulu."

"She certain is a determined woman." Percy grinned. "Her only fault is a shy reluctance to express an opinion." His voice softened. "Sorry you lost your parents."

The boy's face darkened. "No loss. Me and Tug didn't measure up to their standards. Maybe it'll work out better. Sir, I appreciate your coming to this hellhole to give me the news."

"Just doing my job." Percy recalled something. "Say, several year ago, wasn't you the rascal that throwed a stone at a school, busted a window, and distressed our principal?"

"Guilty." Dockery stood up taller. "But I had cause and I'd willing do it again. Them stinking snobs refuse to take Tugwell for a student. They thunk if'n ya don't talk, ya can't learn. Tug thinks. And also reads. I taught him on nights I wasn't transporting giggle juice.

Or driving the bait car."

"Youngster, you surely git a passel of people irritated. Cut quite a gash through Yazoo City. However, I do observe a kindly concern for your kid brother. I regret that you're here. Deeply so."

"I can take it, sir. My brother is the worry."

"He'll do fine at Mr. Dockery's place."

The boy's eyes fired. "So that's where Tug is. No! It ain't rightful."

"Time's up," O'Grady said. "The prisoner is released from the cooler, and you, Mister Chief of Po-lice, can return to Yazoo. We all got laboring to do here."

Dockery was led away by a guard.

Prior to departing the camp, Chief Sweetbutter drove by a chain gang. Six dirty and sweating men chopped brush with machetes, and were singing a blue groan of despair. Out of the gate, he decided to dig into Dockery's file. Perhaps his sentence could be softened. No young delinquent deserves to be housed among hardened criminals, heartless men who'd gone so many years without women. 'Twould scar a young boy for life. It just wasn't decent.

Besides, it was obvious to Percival that the two Dockery brothers ought to be together. He'd mention such to Judge Singletary.

CHAPTER 8

"Breakfast!"

Sun wasn't up yet, but Aunt Lulu was, clanking a fry pan with a spoon or a fork to bugle me out of bed, dressed and downstairs.

I reported to the kitchen, inhaled a savory smell of hot chow, and saw my great-aunt in a faded blue work shirt, trousers, and boots. She stood beside a black six-griddle Acme American stove. Above it a stack of three white plates in the warming oven.

"Morning, Tug," she sang out. She fetched bacon from a skillet and drained it on newspaper. "Each day of uphill cattle ranching is built around a mountain of a meal. So sit."

I sat.

"My so-called baby brother's not down yet.

That means you and I can gobble the lion's share of the larder, to teach him prompt." She jerked a thumb at the ceiling. "Most every wisp of cow cracking Branch knows, he learnt from me. I got taught by our father, Briar Dockery, who lived and worked harder than frozen sin."

Dumping coffee into a mug, Aunt Lulu planted it under my chin, adding a small milk pitcher and sugar bowl to keep it company.

Opening the oven, she said, "Biscuits up. If you taste one of my sinkers, you'll either gag or put yourself outside half a score. Feather light and lime-rock solid. Help yourself to honey butter and a lick of my homemade guava jelly. From our own bushes. We got three back in the citrus grove. I put this up a year ago. It keeps good."

One of Aunt Lulu's hands worked a spatula while the other cracked near to a dozen eggs into the spitting bacon grease.

"Before you or the chickens were awake," she said, "I paraded myself out to the coop to collect these gems of hen fruit. Tomorrow morning, youngster, it'll be *your* chore. Then and every. And don't deliver 'em dirty. Each egg is to be ragged off cleaner than a cat's mouth. Got it?"

I nodded.

And almost smiled.

My mother had a similar way of holding back a smile. As if she couldn't let loose a feeling, because there was so much sadness inside her. It began when I was three, after the awful thing that happened at this cattle ranch. She slowly changed. It got worse when my father's insurance business failed; Bro got arrested and we moved to Moultrie, Georgia. My mom's main hobby got to be collecting laxatives, or crossing herself, spouting religion like a leaky faucet. Her brain somewhere in the clouds.

But Aunt Lulu was as down-to-earth as a mud puddle.

My grandfather appeared, snatched the third plate from the warming oven, piled it, then ate wordlessly. Why didn't he tell Aunt Lulu her biscuits were like eating flowers? I wanted to.

We also had grits and orange juice. Without chatter, the three of us whacked into breakfast as though Mother Nature had doomed its destruction. We reduced it to crumbs and yellowy egg stains. My great-aunt's coffee was sturdy, hot, and so thick that I near about had to stir it with a hammer. Perhaps she brewed it as a medicine to kill germs or rectify evil.

While munching my fifth biscuit, I studied

the pair of oldsters. Seeing as Bro was in jail, Branch and Lulu added up to my entire family. Without them, I'd probable get crated and shipped off to wherever orphans ought, and stay there until I died. A place with locks on the doors and bars to the windows.

Branch swabbed up the kitchen.

To avoid him, I watched Aunt Lulu saddle the mules, Maude and Theodore. But didn't trust them, even though they looked softer than a song and quieter than horses. I took notice of how Lulu stroked each one. Both wanted more of her. I'd heard mules were ornery kickers and ear-back biters, but Theodore and Maude seemed to be gentle enough. However, as they looked like horses, I kept distant. There were no horses at the Diamond Dee. None that I saw. *No horses. No horses. No. No. No.* My brain kept hollering that it mustn't happen again.

Branch come. Aunt Lulu had already mounted up Theodore, and my grandfather climbed into Maude's saddle. Before they rode off, Aunt Lulu instructed me to follow, on foot, to a strange fenced enclosure.

Wheeling her mule, she said, "Your job's to tend gates. Right yonder. Cows and calfs don't hanker to separate, but time's come to wean.

Branch and I'll drive a bunch in your direction. So ready set."

I waited at the wooden pens. Gray rails, all at angles, plus gates. I couldn't figure why.

Give ol' Branch this, he certain could crack a long leather whip without actual lashing a cow's rump. He popped the whip like a firecracker. As the bunch moved toward me, the whip's cracking spooked about twenty. I guessed ten cows, ten calfs. Obeying Aunt Lulu's arm signal, I opened the master pen, and in they all scooted. Twenty head, two people, and two mules.

"Close it!" Aunt Lulu barked. "Good. Now position yourself at the chute gate. When we cut a calf toward it, jar it open enough to allow him entrance. But don't let his ma follow."

Using a prodder pole, as told, I poked calf after calf into the chute, then through a second gate to another holding pen. Rough work. I'd often see Branch or Aunt Lulu wedge a mule between a cow and calf. As the bulky brood cows resisted the separation, it wasn't a snap job. When all ten calfs were isolated, we turned the cows loose, to moo by themselfs. They did so without cease.

Then we castrated six bull calfs.

Branch trapped and tipped each one on its

flank, knelt a knee on its neck, and clamped a hind leg steady. With her gloves off, Aunt Lulu lifted the other hinder to slit the scrotum. She yanked out both balls, and then allowed the bawling bully (now a steer) to jump up free and bleed clean.

This was just the first bunch. We repeated the process all day long, until I figured we'd penned up all the beefs in Florida. Neither Branch nor Lulu spoke to one another, being too busy whooping at their cattle. Yet they smoothly worked the mules in tandem, as a team; Maude and Theodore knew their duties without rein or spur.

Cows respected both the mules. But I avoided them.

Late afternoon, in the kitchen, Aunt Lulu filled three mugs with a hot steamy drink. Pale green, watery.

"Hot pot likker," she said. "It's the leftover broth when I simmer a mess of collards. So sample it for yourself, Tugwell, as it'll help keep you."

Her green stuff tasted worse'n a boiled frog. Yet every sip improved me more'n a mite. A drink to fit a tough day of pen work.

CHAPTER 9

Lucretia's fingers tightened on the wheel. Asleep in the seat beside her, young Tugwell wasn't aware that they had crossed the state line and were now in Georgia. An unpleasant task had to be faced, not dodged. Nine years old. Nowhere near to manhood, but high time to practice being stout gutted. Earlier, when she told Tug that she'd visited Broda Joe in the prison camp, his face lit like a lantern.

There was no way Tugwell could live with her in Rickapee. Just wasn't room in her tiny house. Besides, it was proper for Tugwell to start assuming cattle ranch work and responsibilities. Add to that, Lucretia had a hunch that Tugwell's presence might help Branch be himself again.

Half an hour later, she said, "Tug. Listen up.

We're coming into Moultrie, so kindly instruct me where you folks been camping for the past two years."

The boy blinked.

"Well, where do I go?"

Tug pointed a finger, straight ahead. Then, after seven or eight blocks, he touched her hand and pointed to the right. Lulu turned. For certain, it wasn't a silk-stocking neighborhood. A sorry section of town populated by trash families with too many children and too little grit.

Tug's finger jabbed at a run-down duplex, a two-family dwelling with a weedy dirt yard and a broken front step. A sign stood outside the unit on the right:

FOR RENT

"This the place?"

He nodded.

Out of the car, they were greeted by a smiling man wearing a cheap suit and a clip-on bow tie, and carrying a notepad. "Good day. You people interested in renting? I'm in charge of several locations on this block. Here's my card.

Claxton's the name. Orbin B. Claxton. If this particular site doesn't tickle your fancy, I got a flock of others and I could— "

"Save your breath. My name is Dockery." She showed her driver's license. "Until two weeks ago, this youngster resided here with his parents, Clemson and Melba May Dockery, now deceased. Just the three of them. His first name is Tugwell. We've motored up from Yazoo City, Florida, to claim to what's legally his'n."

"Uh . . . well, all right I guess. The place ought to be cleared out. Let's go inside so y'all can scout around. I don't have too much time to spend, because— "

"No need. We won't use more'n a minute." In the house, she said, "Tug, go upstairs and gather your clothes and valuables. Nobody else's. Stuff 'em into pillowcases. Then return downstairs, so we can stop at the bank, and leave town."

Mr. Claxton's eyebrows raised. "Deceased, you say?"

"Train accident. The youngster can't speak just yet." Standing in the doorway, Lucretia Louise shook her head, looking at the worn rug, a pink fringed lamp shade with no bulb in the socket, and stained wallpaper. Old newspapers littered one corner. "It isn't luxury. Appears as if Clemson and Melba May had fallen into discomfort."

"Looters," the man almost whispered. "Happens every time. Thugs wander in and take whatever they want."

"They are welcome to it."

Tug bounded down the stairs, blank faced, toting a bulging pillow case. Plus an armload of books. Without pause he continued into the kitchen, searching for something. Whatever it was, Tugwell returned without it, his eyes threatening sorrow.

"Look on the back stoop," Lulu advised. "Check that tan carton, then try the trash can. You might get lucky and whatever it be'll turn up."

It did! Tug came prancing back into the parlor holding a beat-up baseball glove. Several sizes too large for his little hand. Smiling, he pointed at the initials that had been burned on the thumb.

BJD

"Broda Joe's mitt?" she asked.

He nodded.

"And he gave it to you, I bet."

Without answering, Tug clutched the tattered hunk of leather to his chest and slowly turned away, as though he and the baseball glove wanted to be alone.

In a hoarse voice, Lulu said, "I guess we now have all we come to retrieve. Thank you, Mr. Claxton. That marble building we passed on the main street . . . I presume that's the bank?"

"Yes'm. Rumor claims it might fail. Go under. If the deceased have assets, best you get there without delay."

"Will do."

The Moultrie Savings & Trust had absolutely no account under Clemson or Melba Dockery. To the contrary. A woman informed that a Mr. Dockery had applied for a loan and was rejected for lack of collateral. And no references.

It was a long trip home. Lucretia Louise was tired and made herself drive more cautiously. For good reason. Beside her rode silent but priceless cargo.

A boy hugging a baseball glove with both arms.

CHAPTER 10

A dark night. No moon.

As he'd done a dozen times, Broda Joe Dockery had slipped the shackle chain off his bunk and sneaked out of the concrete containment barracks. Only for thirty minutes. A guard would soon bed check, with a flashlight.

Made no sense to run away on foot. Wouldn't get far. Even if he crawled under the front gate or climbed over the high, razor-wire fence, no prisoner could survive in the swamp. Too many alligators and black-nose coral snakes. The camp was centered in thirty square miles of wet death.

Except for the road.

Ah, but there is a way! A risky chance. He'd final figured a clean getaway and not be missed until morning. Tonight, all he needed was a few more strands of wire. Shiny. These he patiently collected in the shadows of the mess hall. Then it happened! The metal shackle around his ankle caught on a root, pulled free, and struck a rusty iron garbage barrel. A sharp noise stabbed the quiet night.

WUFF.

When one of the bloodhounds awakened and barked, Broda Joe held his breath, hoping his heart wouldn't quit. He could hear it thumping. Could the dogs? Would the other bloodhounds wake up, sniff, and detect his odor? If so, they'd all bugle. He'd be caught. Lashed.

Or worse, his bunk would be torn apart and searched. Guards would find his store of secret equipment. He'd never escape or see Tugwell. Why hadn't he wrapped the steel ankle cuff in rags, to muffle any contact sound?

Motionless, he waited, wondering how many minutes until the next bed check. Didn't dare to move his feet and create more noise.

Twice he counted to one hundred. Then, hearing neither guards nor dogs, Broda Joe returned to outside his barracks, squeezed his lean body through the narrow gap of dislodged concrete blocks, replaced them, and crept back to his cot. No light. His fingers fumbled, trying to reattach his leg shackle to the cot's crossbar. He couldn't do it. And a guard was unlocking the door.

He'd have to fake it. Show his foot, and pray that the curious flashlight could not pick up the short unattached chain.

Eyes closed, Bro stopped breathing as the light's beam swept the double row of sleeping convicts. Luckily, the irregularity wasn't spotted, the light went out, and the guard departed. A lock bolted shut again. Bro slowly and silently released a long sigh. After waiting a spell, he stood, stooped, and lifted the cot to insert the nine short strands of wire that this evening's outing had produced. All necessary pieces were now assembled. He again lay on his coarse and smelly bed ticking. Eyes open.

"Tomorrow night," he promised Tug.

And smiled.

CHAPTER 11

"Judge . . . you busy?"

In shirtsleeves, glancing up from a stack of blue papers on his desk, Judge Hannah T. Singletary waved his guest to enter.

"Percival. March yourself right in. Never too busy to receive our vigilant chief of police. Hope you're not here to announce a crime wave in Yazoo City."

"Not in the least, Your Honor. All's tranquil."

"Park your massive bulk in a chair."

"Thanks, but I dassn't dawdle. Due to the recent train accident, we have a young boy in the area, age of nine, who's lost both his parents. Tugwell Dockery. According to our town clerk, he was born right here in Yazoo. Years ago, I recall some dreadfully weird tragedy, west of town, involving the death of several horses on the Dockery beef cattle ranch. Some time after, Mr. and Mrs. Clemson Dockery, now deceased, up and left town, possible due to their older son's arrest. Tugwell's brother, Broda Joe, is eighteen. Already served two years at that county labor camp we laughingly call a correctional facility. A year to go. Seems like two years is ample punishment, especial when a pair of young Dockery boys got so sadly parted."

"What's at issue, Percy?"

"Tugwell's a nice child. He's among kin out at the Diamond Dee cattle ranch, with two elderly people. A difficult grandfather, age seventy, plus a great-aunt who is even more senior. Kind of a straining age gap."

"You figure to connect the brothers."

"I do. Even though Broda Joe earned a raw reputation. There's hope for both those boys, if'n we bring 'em together. No proof, Your Honor. Just a gut feeling we ought to limber the law."

Wiping his glasses, Judge Singletary quietly asked, "How long we known each other, Chief?"

"Considerable. Ever since we was both squirming under the witchcrafty eye of Miss Murgatroid."

"This is the first favor you requested of me."

Percy nodded, and then smiled. "Enough a reason to grant it?"

"A judicial pardon?"

"Please."

"Years ago, I did meet the Dockery family somewhere. Seem decent folks. You personally know these two lads?"

"Lately met both. Our nine-year-old doesn't speak. The impact of that freight train shocked him silent. Might run deeper than that. Who knows? But I got a notion the older kid could ease him out of it."

Hooking thumbs into flowered suspenders. Judge Singletary gazed at the ceiling as if seeking guidance from the yellowing plaster. Percy held his breath.

"Dockery. I do recall sentencing that young rascal for trafficking alcohol, prohibited by the Volstead Act. Driving the decoy car a mile ahead of a shipment."

"Agreed. He's a scamp. Also busted a school window, but in a rather noble cause. My guess is that he run booze for a like reason. Because of his brother." Percy shrugged his beefy shoulders. "Just a hunch."

Judge Singletary cracked his knuckles, one

by one. "A pardon can prove risky. My appellate brethren in Tallahassee have frowned more than once in our direction. However . . ." The Judge stood. "Percival, you'd make a clever courtroom attorney, swaying a jury as you have persuaded me."

"Your Honor does me too much credit."

Checking his gold pocket watch, Judge Singletary said, "I'm late for a pretrial. But you'll have that pardon release, in writing, by early next week."

They shook hands.

Chief Sweetbutter wasn't exactly the build for dancing. Yet, leaving the judicial chambers, Percy attempted a modest buck and wing. Only one.

Fred Astaire might get jealous.

CHAPTER 12

He coughed.

Although beaten down by work, Broda Joe couldn't sleep.

So he lay in the dark, inside a cement-block containment with its padlocked door, listening to nine other convicts snore. Smelling their unwashed stink. Beyond the single window and its iron bars, frogs croaked in the swamp mist. An owl hooted its hunger.

Tonight?

Yes, he would escape this very night. Providing that Captain Ogre O'Grady was entertaining his customary female guest. No sign of her as yet. No pink car.

For almost a year, Broda Joe Dockery had made plans. And prepared, gathering gray tufts of soiled mattress stuffing, rags, a discarded white tick that had held dried corn husks. Hiding items up the hollow cot legs. Above all, he'd been patient. But now he could wait no longer, not with Tugwell at Branch's. Not after what happened six years ago.

Bro couldn't help recalling that prior to the horrid incident, Grampap had been a good guy. Nevertheless, his kid brother be terrified of that man, and might run away somewhere. Thus his decision. Tonight! Not for his own freedom, but to free Tug.

"Tugwell, your cage is tighter than mine."

Underneath his bunk were two items. A small bundle of clothes. And a strange hunk of dried wood, pale tan, bleached almost white by the sun. The wood fiber was soft, light, and Bro guessed it was tupelo. He'd found it and saved it, because it reminded him of a human foot, complete with half a lower leg. Broda Joe had spent hours working on the wood sculpture, refining its shape by using shards of glass from a broken bottle. It took time, yet his third foot gradually sprouted toes. He braided wire strands into chain links, plus an ankle shackle.

Lying awake, waiting, hoping, he at last heard the woman's car! No way he could see it from here. But on the nights Tarla Fernando came to visit O'Grady, always the laboring engine followed by the same silly giggle to greet the Boss Man.

He knew Ogre wanted the prisoners to hear her. They were men without women, hearing them together, sounds of Ogre and her drinking hooch. Lustful grunts of pleasure, or displeasure. They were envious of his guttery laugh and his store-bought cigarettes.

A steel cuff shackled Broda Joe's ankle to the cot. A horizontal crossbar prevented the chain's loop from falling to the floor. Only Bro knew how he had loosened the crossbar, by continuous taps and twists. Easing the crossbar from its socket, he softly slid the steel loop onto the dirt floor, and then lifted the bed a inch.

He was free.

Nothing new. He'd done so repeatedly, sneaking to the corner to remove two concrete blocks, slipping his skinny body outside again and again. Yet this time, before squeezing himself outside and repositioning the blocks, he wadded the mattress stuffing and rags into a human shape, hiding it beneath his blanket.

Only a foot would show. A wooden foot.

Around its ankle a fake shackle made of wire strands.

No sweat. When a guard's flashlight checked bed after bed, no vacated cot. No escape siren would violate the night with its scream. Over a two-year period, Broda Joe had heard its warning wail several times. The bloodhounds, after being allowed to sniff the deserted bunk, eagerly howled with the sport of a fresh scent and bugled in glee when the helpless convict was overtaken. Caught. Then a distant gunshot.

Broda Joe wouldn't stupidly crawl under the barbed wire and wade into wet, to meet up a gator or a cottonmouth. Stealing a horse wouldn't do. Not over razor wire ten foot high.

There was a wiser way.

Tarla's car.

Weeks ago, groping in the dark, he had searched its interior for a place to hide. No dice. Crawling underneath, Bro tried to cling to the tailpipe or axle, to suspend himself off the ground. But weak from a lack of food, he could hang beneath her car only half a minute. Possible less. Too short a time.

How else could he use it?

Unwittingly, his fellow inmates supplied the

answer. Due to his youth and nearly nonexistent facial hair, they called Bro "Girlie Face," saying he favored O'Grady's hot blonde boopsie.

A month ago, after a loud and cussing argument with Ogre, Tarla was fixing to leave. A fight ensued. O'Grady tried to tear her white lace collar. Tarla hit him with her purse, and the contents fell out. All was retrieved except a tiny lipstick. Outside that night, Bro found it and kept it inside the hollow cot leg.

During this slapping battle between the woman and her heavy host, Broda Joe made another key discovery.

Tarla Fernando was not a blonde!

O'Grady had snatched a wig from her head, waved it around, and placed it on his own baldness. Falling down drunk, he tried to rip it. Annoyed enough to spit tacks, Tarla fled to her car and roared off toward the exit gate. Alone, polishing off a jug of booze, O'Grady passed out cold. Broda Joe had stolen the blonde wig along with the lipstick and returned to his containment house to reshackle his ankle and fall asleep.

On the following night, as others slept, Broda Joe used a rusty razor blade to transform a scrap of bed ticking into a fancy ring of white cloth.

Around his neck, in darkness, it could pass for a white lace collar.

At last he was ready. Tonight!

He sneaked outside the containment barracks for a final time, moving through the shadows, being careful that the now-useless chain and shackle around his ankle didn't strike any metal. From inside Ogre O'Grady's bedroom, there came muffled laughter, and then the usual moaning, followed by easier breathing, and eventual stillness.

Earlier, in haste, Tarla had draped her flaming orange coat carelessly on an outside chair. On tiptoe, Bro snatched it. Now wearing the coat, a white lace collar, a beat-up blonde wig, and lipsticked lips, Broda Joe pushed Tarla's car noiselessly down a gentle slope and toward the front gate. When he could push no longer, he slipped behind the steering wheel.

To hot-wire a motor was no hurdle.

Praying that neither Tarla nor O'Grady heard the choking engine in low gear, he approached the gate. Creaking on its ungreased hinges, it swung open. As the car rolled through, the sleepy guard mumbled a foul suggestion. He probable expected no answer.

Broda Joe, however, couldn't resist tossing him a farewell crumb. An imitation of Tarla's giggle.

Shifting gears into second, then high, the twin sister of a very cooperative Tarla Fernando left the Pecan County Correctional Labor Camp without a twinge of regret. Now wigless, he whispered to the damp Florida night.

"Hang on, Tug. Your brother's coming."

CHAPTER 13

Early.

No sun, and no breakfast.

My aunt, so she said, wasn't partial to my upchucking on her. As we walked toward the corral, Aunt Lulu explained. She and I were fixing to ride Theodore together. The thought of being aboard a big strong animal that looked close to a horse almost made me puke in fear. My lips trembled. A fluttering in my belly, and I had a notion to turn around and run away.

Please. I don't want to do this.

Before today, I hadn't rid a animal, and I knew that I would never ride a horse. Or touch one. But seeing as Aunt Lulu had done so much for my benefit, I got up my guts and mounted the mule.

Instead of forking a saddle, we rode bareback. She in back, I was in front. No bridle or bit. Theodore toted a loose halter, no ribbons—merely two thick lead ropes, knotted ends, and pressure from Aunt Lulu's trousered knees.

We rode Theodore for about a mile in the early-morning mist. Not much to look at, until we passed a place beside a small pond where the soft ground had been roughed.

"See there, Tugwell? A wild boar do that. My dear daddy called it a piney-wood rooter. That tore-up ground got caused by his snout searching for grubs, roots, or even mice. Some hogs grow to be enormous. Seen several over five hundred pound. Yet give the porky devils their due. They don't do near as much harm to our herd as coyotes."

Theodore kept at a slow walk.

No bulls. Only a passel of white-face brood cows with long horns that had recent dropped calfs. Some, I figured, during the night. A bloodied thing was dangling from the underbelly of a calf that stood on unsteady legs. Still wet from birthing. A cow licked its face.

What's that? Wondering about it, I pointed.

"Oh, that there string is a umbilical cord. Attaches a mother to a baby. In a couple three days, it'll atrophy, dry up, and fall off. As a infant, you had one yourself."

Doubting, I looked up at her over my shoulder.

"That's how come you have a belly button. Everybody's owned one since time began. With the possible exception of Adam and Eve."

Her joke lightened me, sudden aware that my downhearted face hadn't cracked a grin since the train. Losing my parents made me feel double empty. I'd truly tried to love them. But they'd turned their backs on Broda Joe and hardly spoke to me, knowing they'd get no reply. When Bro packed off to prison and we moved to Georgia, our family life turned colder than stone. I couldn't write a letter to my brother because my folks wouldn't give me his labor camp address. So I walked around wanting to die. Often skipping my special-class school.

Last night, had me a itch to run away to find Bro. However, it didn't seem rightful to disappear and frighten Aunt Lulu. The shock could keel her over.

But I have to see my brother! I can't take another year alone.

At his own speed, Theodore plodded slow and even among another scattered bunch of cows, none of which paid us heed. We never dismounted. We saw bloody turf beneath the mangled remains of a fresh calf.

"Coys," Aunt Lucretia Louise growled. "Coydogs. Coyotes. Heard 'em last night. Woke me up, and at first blink I reckoned wolfs. But coyotes yip instead of yowl." Pulling Theodore to a halt, she said, "Coyotes survive in all forty-eight states, so I heard tell. Over the decades, Branch and I tried every ruse short of all-out witchcraft to rid 'em." She shrugged. "Nothing seems to spook 'em off the Diamond Dee."

Aunt Lulu turned the mule.

"Tugwell, let's point home. We seen our purpose. Branch was up half the night outdoors in his nightshirt with a Winchester, hoping he'd knock down a coyote. Let's nudge him awake and eat us a bodacious breakfast."

Approaching the house, we rode along a slight hump of land that was new to me. A grassy knoll. A blackjack oak and a pecan tree shaded its summit; beneath, four white picket fences formed a small square. Inside lay a trio of graves, each with its own hand-carved wooden marker. Weathered to gray.

"Tugwell, this is our family plot." Pointing to each, she said, "My father, Briar Luke Dockery.

My mother, Eudora. The third covers my sweet and loving sister-in-law, Aloma Ruth Tugwell Dockery." Aunt Lulu sighed. "Your grandmother." Her voice became a bit scratchy. "As you possible don't remember, Aloma Ruth was my brother's dear wife, whom he adored, and who died in horrible fashion. Six years ago."

I couldn't breathe.

Eyes clamped shut, I hoped that my great-aunt wouldn't whoa Theodore to a halt. Yet that's what she did.

"Someday," she said softly, "I'll be buried here. So will Branch. I intend to lie eternal with my brother and Aloma Ruth." Behind me, I felt Aunt Lulu's body stiffen as though turning to timber. "Later, after a full lifetime, you and Broda Joe will be buried beside us. Dockerys rest in Dockery land."

Don't tell me no more. Not about my grandmother's dying, or old Branch and the awful things he done. I hate him.

How I wanted to yell all of this at Aunt Lulu, yet couldn't. Words were screaming inside my ears. Back at the corral, I kicked myself off the mule real quick, not bearing to look at the animal because he looked too much like a horse.

I didn't want Branch to hurt Theodore.

CHAPTER 14

Whoop. Whoop. Whoop. Whoop. Whoop . . .

Forcing his underslept eyes to open, Walter Patrick O'Grady couldn't tolerate the wail of the camp's warning siren. Guards shouting. The bloodhounds barking like crazy. All of them noises total up to one mess.

A bird had flied away!

Beaten in brain and body by last evening's booze, Ogre O'Grady roll his person from bed, reaching an unsteady hand for extra-large gray longjohn. His underwear suit. Thrusted a fat foot into it, then another, and tried to locate a sleeve. Twisted thing! Like somebody tie it in a knot.

Ogre cussed a purple fit. Howsomever, in the artistic use of profanity, he couldn't begin to equal the language of a woman who just discover that, in the night, her car got stole.

Not to mention a orange coat.

Now a redhead, and swearing up a storm, Tarla Fernando was fully dressed. She chased him to a nearby cement-block barracks, calling him every name in the book. A string of old favorites plus a few more she invent. As he run, O'Grady try to pull on a shirt, almost trip and fall, realizing that his long underwear was on backward.

Tarla kept whacking him with a mop handle until he snatch it from her and busted it against his knee.

Wasn't much of a morning yet. Inside the dimly lit containment shelter, nine bunks still held their ankle-cuffed prisoners. Some in stripes. Others near to naked. The tenth bunk lay empty. It display a odd hunk . . . of what? To O'Grady it feel like tupelo wood. Or bass. Shape like a human's foot, the pesky thing be sort of fixed to a foot rail by a fake chain, flimsy, made of thin metal strips. Wires.

All of it phony.

Soon's he yank the foot free, turning, exiting the building and in disbelief showing it to Tarla, she scream at him, "*Stupido. Tonto.* My car she is gone. Losted. And you find me *foot*?"

Three of the guards was hollering, dogs yowled, Tarla continue to cuss him out. The damnable siren kept on a *whoop whoop whooping* . . . until Ogre thunk his hurtful head fix to explode. Worse of all, the prisoners was pointing his way and laughing at him. No doubt thinking him a fool.

"My car, Walter. Go get!" Snatching the wooden foot out of his hand, Tarla whacked him across the face.

"Quit," he yelped. "And will one a you idiots turn the dang siren off, afore it drive me sane."

"Stupido ox." Tarla also added a few fresh phrases that, to Captain O'Grady, didn't exact ring favorable.

Grabbing the shirtfront of the closest night guard in a firm fist, Ogre snarl, "Who? Tell me now. Which 'n git away gone?"

"Dockery."

"Curse his eyes." Ogre chewed his lip. "Go fetch the hounds. Bring 'em in here to sniff his bunk as a starter. Them bloods is all smart, Tarla. They'll track him to a fall down. I vow."

This promise didn't seem to soothe the ruffled

feathers of Tarla Fernando or her redheaded temper. She spat in his face.

"Dog is smarter than you," she yelped. "How they smell *car*?"

CHAPTER 15

Branch Dockery awoke.

The bedside clock said eight-thirty, as if scolding. Shameful late for a rancher who usual rolled out at five. Painful stiff, he reached for a tired boot, one that was still a bit warm.

Downstairs, he found no one about. As the stove wasn't hot, Branch reckoned that a breakfast had neither been cooked nor forked. Outside the kitchen door, he noticed, one of the mules was missing. Lucretia Louise had probable taken the child for a morning ride on Theodore. Maude came to him for a hug. As she trustingly rested her head on his shoulder, he kissed her soft gray muzzle. What a loyal animal.

"Good morning, girl."

While awaiting their return, he'd pay visit to

the cemetery. He did so every day, often at sundown, for a moment alone with his Aloma Ruth. To kneel. Touch the earth that held her. She'd forever be his heart's bouquet. As was his custom, Branch stood solemnly at her grave on the knoll, removed his hat, closed his eyes, and prayed for her eternal rest.

Decades ago, a pretty Miss Aloma Ruth Tugwell had been the only young lady to twinkle his eye. At the Sunday afternoon church picnic, beneath a magnolia tree, she agreed to become his bride.

When they kissed for the first time, she tasted sweeter than cider. They fitted closer than stacked spoons. Staring at the graves of his parents, he recalled how they had passed away early.

Branch and Lucretia Louise were working the ranch as partners. Even then, his older sister was bossy. But when Branch married, Lucretia graciously moved into town, to Yazoo, and later to Rickapee. Yet she visited them often.

It was Paradise.

The two young women became like sisters, sharing recipes and sewing patterns, singing duets, and whispering secrets. Some were jokes at his expense. Aloma Ruth was the person who shortened Lucretia Louise's name to Lulu. It stuck.

Lulu had been present, in the upstairs bedroom, during that long night when Aloma nearly died in childbirth. After waiting so long to become pregnant, his wife had been more fearful of the baby's life than of losing her own.

A boy was born.

Clemson Dockery would be their only blessing. Aloma could bear no more children, they were informed.

As years passed, Clem didn't grow up sturdy. He was plain lazy. Couldn't pinch dirt out a post hole. Unfit for Florida's outback, he couldn't ride, rope, hot brand, or castrate calfs. Or even capon a cockerel. What he could do was play poker, shoot dice, and soak up swill from a bottle.

Like a dope, he got a girl in trouble.

Clemson was forced to marry Melba May Broda.

As all Melba May wanted to discuss was religion, Branch avoided her. He did, however, treat her cordial, persuaded by Aloma Ruth, who befriended everyone.

"Not just people," Branch whispered to her grave. "You respected every life, be it man, woman, child, cow, or a yellow baby chick. Whenever your fingertip touched a leaf, the entire plant responded in bloom."

Until . . . that day!

By then, he and Aloma were the grandparents of two boys, ages twelve and three. Clem and Melba dropped them off at the ranch and went motoring. On errands. Tuckered out from a baseball game, Broda Joe needed a nap. Aloma was outside at the corral with little Tugwell, showing him how to saddle a horse. He was a black-strap brown. Three other horses were also in the pen.

Who knows how it started. . . .

As her small grandson watched, Aloma Ruth became a sudden victim. Napoleon, a bay gelding who adored her, turned to bite her neck. She fell, bleeding, and the horse must have kicked her head. Branch was indoors and heard the commotion. Dashing from the house, he saw Aloma's lacerated neck and crushed skull. Ears back, Napoleon stood over her body.

Kneeling, Branch tried to revive his wife. The damage was too severe. Aloma Ruth's face had drained to a ghostly white.

Revenge flooded him.

Insane with grief, he grabbed an ax. Then, one by one, he cracked the gelding's legs. Unable to stop, he hacked at leg after leg until four horses fell in a whinny of fear and agony. The ax blade did not rest. All four throats were cut. Their suffering cries silenced by death. Never again, Branch swore an oath, would the hoof of a horse tread the Diamond Dee domain. If so, the horse would be slaughtered.

Gasping, heart pounding, he was aware that his clothing, now stained a dark crimson with hot horse blood, seemed to be steaming his body. Was he burning in some red Hell?

Had a tiny child witnessed his madness?

Standing among family graves and feeling so shattered by what his rage had done, the guilt jolted Branch Dockery out of his past. When a man loses control, he loses so much more. He had begun to destroy his family. One by one. Clemson, Melba May, Broda Joe, and finally Tugwell.

How long could he maintain any affection with Lucretia Louise? Or his grandsons? At present, it was a strain to think positive about Broda Joe. This cut-uppity had constantly been in trouble, afoul of the law, now in jail. Perhaps always would be, for one felony or another. Then, on the other hand, Tugwell, who cannot speak. Having seen a horror no child deserves to see.

Would it scar him forever? It should not. Tugwell was only nine years old, and his wounded childhood deserved to be patched up whole. Lucretia had certain done her part. No reason for her to shoulder the entire burden. Burden? No. 'Twould be a honor to pitch in and help the hurting of a fine little boy.

Branch knew he'd once been a decent man, with family and friends. Neighbors. About time he emerged from his dungeon. He couldn't bring back his beloved Aloma Ruth. Yet he might help to heal a grandchild who bore her maiden name.

Tugwell.

CHAPTER 16

Tug.

The name made Broda Joe happy.

A pity he'd reunite with Tugwell as a runaway con. Better than not seeing him at all. With luck, he could reach the Diamond Dee by afternoon. His first stop, however, would be a backstreet in Yazoo City, a repair place where cars got repainted.

No light in the shop.

Gil's Garage didn't open quite this early. So, parked in the unlit alley, he cut the engine. Exhausted, he slept. Until a hand roughly shook his shoulder. In panic, his eyes popped open to see a familiar face.

"Wake up, buddy. You can't park here."

"Sure I can. Owner's a friend of mine."

"Holy gazooks." Gil Gilbarton blinked. "Is that *you*, Bro Joe?"

He coughed. "What's left of me."

"I heared you was . . . inside."

"*Was.*"

Gil shook a wrinkled and unshaved face. "What in thunder you doing in Tarla Fernando's car? Don't tell me. I'd wager you and this vehicle is both hot. And wanted."

"Bull's-eye."

"Young dodger, you're fixing to bestow me a heap of hassle. Aiding and abetting somebody on the lam." Gil stopped to consider. "Looks to me like you ain't been eating regular. Ya lost weight. Hungry?"

Bro nodded.

"Thelma comes at seven. Brews coffee. She usual brings hot rolls or doughnuts from a all-night bakery where my granddaughter works." Gil studied the car. "Best we drape a tarp over this pink crate. Here to Yazoo, every dude in town knows these wheels. And recognize that you ain't built like its owner."

"Can you paint it, Gil? . . . I can't pay."

"No matter. Soon's my helpers git here, we'll give it a whole new personality, for old time's sake. Call it a coming-out present."

Thelma Granberry arrived, saw Bro at the car, winked, but never said boo. People who worked for Gil kept their lips sealed, as one of Gil's special services was altering a car's color. Often at night. He also supplied souped-up speed for hauling hooch and outdistancing deputies. That's how, two years ago, Gil and Broda Joe knew one another.

Bro feasted on jelly doughnuts and java, then rested while Gil Gilbarton and two sleepy Mexicans painted a pink car black. Plus welding. The job took several hours.

"Conspicuous," Gil said. "Now ain't that a uppity word? Means easy to identify. Not by color, by outline, in spite of the fresh plates and bumpers. Wait'll you catch my next move."

He added jeweled mud flaps and a sporty pair of artificial foxtails to the twin overhead antennas. Like banners to wave in the breeze.

"Got extra," he said. "So sit tight."

Fishing into a messy desk drawer, Gil produced a slip of paper. A list of possible sayings to stencil on the black car, so it would appear to be owned by some schoolboy hotshot.

OH YOU KID
BORED OF EDUCATION

LET'S MAKE WHOOPEE
YHS . . . FOR YAZOO HIGH SCHOOL
DON'T LAUGH. YOUR DAUGHTER'S INSIDE.

"So," said Gil, "we print one or two of these here smarty-pants yukkers on the doors, maybe on the hood or roof. Not even Tarla would know what it used to be."

This they did. Also the steering wheel had a new fake-fur cover.

"Sonny," Gil asked, "how bad do you gotta drive illegal wheels around Pecan County, like you're itching to return to the comforts of the labor camp?"

"I can't go back, Gil." Bro shuddered. "I'd die first."

"Ugly place?"

"Guards are mean enough. The other cons are much worse. The ringleader is Zaggert. Us prisoners call him the Critter. He's more feared than O'Grady. I been shamed. Them gorillas took my self-respect. My dignity. I got used awful bad, Gil. Before I'd go back, I'd rather hang. A hanging's only once. What Zaggert and his gang done at me was most every day."

"God," his friend said, as though in prayer, "I won't let you go back." Gil snapped his blackened fingers. "We'll work a deal with these Mex boys and their relatives. A fair shake. They's eager to own wheels. We'll use the wrecker and haul it over to their neighborhood. I got skeleton keys that'll fit the ignition."

Bro nodded. "When can we start?"

Eyeing the shackle on his ankle, Gil said, "Soon's I hammer a chisel to cut that infernal jewelry off'n you."

He did so.

"Here," Gil said. "Want a souvenir? Tote it along. Might serve to remind you to keep your sorry butt a hundred miles from O'Grady and his Pecan County hospitality. And pursue a honest living. For yourself, and that kid brother you always brag about."

"Thanks, Gil. I owe ya. Keep it for laughs."

A few hours later, Broda Joe Dockery was no longer connected to a leg iron, prison-issue shoes, or Tarla's formerly pink machine.

As Gil said, the Mexicans turned out to be more'n polite. A few had been O'Grady inmates and laughed like hyenas hearing about the getaway, wanting to even a score. In exchange for Tarla's car, Broda Joe was given plenty of spicy food inside a tortilla, wine, sandals, a white cotton shirt and white baggy trousers worn by field pickers, and a floppy straw sombrero. And forty-nine dollars in cash money. Best of all, a hot soapy bath, hair and all.

Plus a strange new form of transportation.

That afternoon he rode west, clip-clopping in the direction of the Dockery Diamond Dee cattle ranch. Moving so slowly that nobody would notice one more Mexican.

He'd let Tugwell name the donkey.

CHAPTER 17

"Boys," ordered Aunt Lulu, "sit yourselfs."

As commanded, Branch and I sat at the kitchen table with its faded pink oilcloth. After riding Theodore bareback, I'd washed up at the sink with brown laundry soap. My great-aunt acted a bit limpy in the legs. At the stove, she held her fingers close to a front griddle, for heat.

"Arthritis," she explained. "Morning's the worst time. Joints are stiffer than a Methodist sermon. My backbone feels like I been run over by a slow wagon."

Saying nothing, Branch left the table to poke around in a lower cupboard and brought out a small bottle. Uncorking it, he rubbed some of its smelly contents on his sister's hands.

"Turp?" she asked him.

"A tincture of turpentine, vinegar, and castor oil."

"What warlock concocted *that*?"

"Me," Branch grunted. "Try a rub of this mix, plus a bee sting or two. Won't cure arthritis. Nothing's ever cured mine. Yet it'll check it to tolerable. And help your walking so's you won't have a hitch in your gitalong."

Branch was as sour as a kumquat. For certain, I'd made up my mind not to trust the old devil. And that went double if'n he was anywhere near a ax! However, Aunt Lulu had asked me to give my grandfather a chance. Maybe a fresh start. I was taken aback to learn that grumpy Branch Dockery actual cared about somebody.

Well, it proved to be a morning of surprises.

"Boy," he said at me, "there's a chore that begs doing. Can't quite handle it lonesome. Maybe you'd cotton to help?"

I cautiously nodded.

"Good lad."

Aunt Lulu, dumping hot onion eggs on our plates, said nothing, her eyebrow raised.

Turned out, we loaded a collection of tools, hardware, a small sack of corn kernels, and bit of lumber into a wagon bin. From the tack room, Branch brung a pair of dark leather collars for Maude and Theodore.

"Take notice," he told me, "that a collar has to fit proper. The collar's bottom needs room to allow a man's hand between a mule's neck and the leather. Two inches. Or else it'll cramp the animal's windpipe."

Heading for the pine woods to the south, Branch held the reins. But a ways out, he handed the black leather ribbons to me and said, "You drive."

Wasn't a lot of driving to do.

Our mules seemed to sense where we was going, and went there. They had observed and smelled what we loaded into the wagon, including the corn bag. Might be that Theodore and Maude and I were distant cousins. I figured all three of us knowed things we didn't yap about.

Before my brother got sent off to the labor camp, Bro told me I was smart. The test was a lead-pipe cinch. Broda Joe read me a story about a boy named Tom Sawyer. He let me read some of it as we went along. At the end, he asked me who this Tom lived with . . . a father, mother, or a aunt?

Soon as he said "aunt," I smiled.

"Did he whitewash a wall, a house, or a fence?" To answer, I held up ten fingers, like pickets, and Bro clapped my shoulder. "Be patient, Tug. Just keep reading the books I bring ya. Store the learning, and it'll pay off. You will someday show that entire schoolhouse. You'll teach *them* a trick."

Another good thing I remembered about Bro. He found a book we'd took out from the Yazoo City Free Library. Long overdue.

"Borrowing a book, Tug, is sort of like a handshake. We made a promise to bring it back. That's how honest guys do."

Returning *The Wind in the Willows* to our public library was one of the last things that Broda Joe and I did together, before they packed him off to prison. And my parents and I left Yazoo to live in Moultrie, Georgia.

Without as much as a twitch on the reins, Maude and Theodore stopped and stood still. Trees were all around us. Pines, oaks, and cedar.

"We're here," Branch told me.

Nearby was a funny-looking geegaw constructed of gray boards, chicken wire, and several sturdy corner posts. Sure wasn't a hen coop, because no wire stretched across the top. Whatever was intended to be inside didn't have wings. As he worked the door entrance up and down, Branch scowled.

"Drat. The rooters parade right in, gobble up

all my corn bait, and then . . . handsome as you please . . . they sashay right out again, and vanish."

Who? I had a itch to ask him. *Is this thing a trap? If you tell me what's it do, I can help you repair it.*

As though he heard me, my grandfather talked about his doo-funny, why it was there, and what it got built for. To catch hogs. "Right after you got born, little Broda Joe and I rigged this thing together. Some of our pigs wandered loose. Went feral. Enough wild hogs here on this property to sausage all of Florida. So nowadays instead of raising, we trap 'em."

I pointed at the see-through shanty.

"Yup," he said. "That's my pig trap. Trouble is, it don't seem to function right. Let's reason why not."

It hurt his spine to bend, Branch said, and that was why he often limped. So I crawled inside through the vertical trap door, and it was easy to see why it wasn't falling. The trigger was half a broomstick, round and horizontal. When the door was up and open, it was held by a pair of nails on the yonder side of two uprights, a yard apart. The nails weren't in the stick but under it, and were too long and bent down so the trap couldn't spring. The wrong kind of nails, as their heads were too large. Almost dimes.

Bro had showed me how to work tools and hardware, so this chore weren't going to be any trouble.

All this trap needed was a pair of new nails, and a claw hammer. These I went to the wagon to fetch. Back inside, I let the door down with a bang. Prying the nails free, I pounded in two brads. Headless nails.

Took all my weight to pull the trigger rope to raise the gate. But did. I motioned for Branch to watch me scatter corn under the broomstick, which was eight inches above the ground. Then, down on all fours, pretending to eat the corn as a pig would, I gave the stick a gentle head nudge.

Wham!

The trap door dropped. Snorting like a captured hog, I looked at my grandfather. Branch didn't say anything. But as he lifted the trap door to let me free, I could tell he was pleased, because he looked square at me and mussed my hair. He didn't fool me. Old Branch already knowed what ailed the trap, but he just wanted me to learn for myself.

Back at the house, Branch opened up and told Aunt Lucretia Louise about what a troubleshooter I was, and that I fixed and reset the trap like another Mr. Thomas Alva Edison.

My reward was a pencil. A fancy one. It was a bright red with yellow stripes and a brass belt to clinch the eraser. It was the very first blunt-ended new pencil I'd ever got. Cracking open his pocket jackknife, my grandfather shaved and sharped it, exposing the lead to a point.

Handing it back to me, he said, "On most every pencil there's a eraser. Why? Because us humans all make mistakes that ought to git corrected. Years ago I made one. When your grandma, Aloma Ruth, got killt by a horse, it cut deep. Twisted me into a deranged devil." Tapping my hand with my new pencil, he said, "Help me erase my mistake, begin anew, and be your grampap."

Taking my new pencil in one hand, I touched his hand with the other, to let Grampap know that I wasn't so afeared of him. Then I used my new pencil to print THANK YOU. It made old Branch smile.

With a dish towel over her shoulder, Aunt Lulu noticed the pair of us menfolks together, now sort of a team, the way Maude and Theodore pulled a wagon.

"Step at a time," she said.

CHAPTER 18

It wasn't quite supper time.

Sitting sideways in the front porch double-seater swing, knees up, I was reading a book Bro gave me, before going away.

Cash Boy by Mr. Horatio Alger.

Next I was fixing to read *Bob Burton*. He gave me that, too. Broda Joe said I'd like the way Mr. Alger's stories end. If a fellow keep honest and hard-working, he'd be rewarded. And good things would happen.

Glancing up from page 33, I spotted something unusual in the distance. A white speck. Moving, and growing bigger. A boy on a burro? A floppy straw hat was hiding his face. Maybe a Mex. For sure, they were coming toward the house. Giving *Cash Boy* a rest, I stood up and walked forward.

He waved.

Why are you waving your hat? You don't know me and I never seen you before. I don't know any of the Mexican people. . . . What are you yelling?

"Tug! Tugboat!"

Just one person called me Tugboat. Hearing it, I sudden knew, and the sweet sound of it went right through me, ringing my heart like a bell.

Bro! Bro! Broda Joe!

Even though I made no sound, my brother would hear. Always could. Bro had special ears. Barefoot, I was running and couldn't stop. Bro jumped off the donkey and then he was running, too. Close, and closer, until his skinny arms went around me, squeezing life into me. Holding on. So he wouldn't get away again.

"Tug." He could barely talk. "Little guy, I missed you so much. But don't ask what a labor camp is like. I can't tell nobody. Not even you. I had to bust loose, Tug, to come see you. Find out if you're okay here. Safe. And proper fed."

Hang tight to me, Bro. Please don't never let go. You can hear me. Tell me, Bro. Say that you still hear as you used to.

"I hear ya. Our secret is because we listen.

Most folks don't. And I won't stop hearing everything you tell me. So keep talking, pal. I'm here. And I brung my ears."

Bro . . . Bro . . .

Over and over, I kept on saying his name, longing to hear him say Tugboat. *Hear me. I am a real person, not just a dumb thing that can't speak. Or go to a regular school.*

Two years had went by. Bro was eighteen now, but he certain hadn't growed much. Maybe a inch. Broda Joe never had been chubby, but now he was closer to a skeleton. Even his eyes looked empty. But he was here. It made me feel like shouting.

"Hey, guess what? I brung you a new friend to talk to. She's a donkey. Cuter than candy, and your perfect size. See?"

Opening my eyes, I saw a furry gray animal with long floppy ears. She slowly walked to us like we were hers.

What's her name?

"I got her a few hours ago. Call it a swap. She doesn't talk a word. But she's to be all yours." Bro scratched his head. "Trouble is, she don't got a name."

Right then, it didn't matter.

"Give her a hug. Gentle. That's right, throw

your arms around her neck and feel how scratchy she be. Yet inside, she's all candy."

Hearing a screen door open and close, I turned to see Aunt Lulu and Grampap standing on the porch. Staring, as though they couldn't believe the scene.

Bro's here. He's to home!

As they neared us, my brother coughed and then spoke up quick. "Don't worry. I can't stay. Guess you can figure why. Diamond Dee will be the first place police'll come searching."

"You're so thin," Aunt Lulu said, holding him close to her. "Nothing but a bag of bones."

"Broda, come inside," Grampap said, "where we can feed you. Looks like you could also use a night's rest."

Can't stay? Bro can't stay? He said he'd be leaving again. Going away? *No! You can't go, Bro. If you go, I'm going with you. To wherever. We won't be afraid or poor. We'll be brothers.*

Bro shook his head at Grampap and Aunt Lulu. "Anyplace I go, I bring trouble. That's why my parents had to leave Yazoo and locate to Georgia. Couldn't take the shame. Pa blamed me that his insurance business fell apart. It was like they didn't have me no more as a son." He sighed. "The train accident wasn't their fault. It was mine. I made 'em move to Moultrie."

"Let's not stand out here," Aunt Lulu said. "I have supper on the stove and it might burn." She took Bro by the arm. He seemed too tired to argue.

Grampap said, "Tugwell, let's you and me escort the donkey to some grain and water." To Lulu, he said, "We'll be inside soon to wash up."

All I could think about was that Bro would be leaving again. It cut like a knife. Everyone, including the donkey, moved. Except me. My feet wouldn't budge.

Like a stake, I'd got pounded into the ground.

CHAPTER 19

Percival Sweetbutter whistled a tune.

Atop a cypress tree, a mockingbird was trilling a variety of good-morning happiness. It promise to be a sunshiner.

Exiting the Yazoo City patrol vehicle, his mood almost made him skip, as the chief of police walked merrily toward the Pecan County Correctional Labor Camp office. He was carrying a blue-wrapped legal document, signed and sealed by Judge Hannah T. Singletary.

A pardon for young Broda Joe Dockery.

Be a genuine pleasure to reunite brothers, especially a pair so heavy loaded by problems.

Earlier, in town, the chief had received a surprise visit from one of Yazoo's most spectacular citizens. Tarla Fernando was outraged that her missing automobile hadn't yet been recovered. O'Grady, she reported, had pleaded with her not to report the incident, promising to handle it himself. Without publicity. Miss Tarla was through waiting. The details she supplied were punctuated by words that couldn't be repeated verbatim in the record. Several would have made a sailor blush.

In broken English and Spanish, she offered a few particulars of an escape, yet couldn't remember the convict's name. Her description of Ogre O'Grady with his long underwear on backwards tested Percy's ability to maintain a sober face.

Up the outside steps he bounded, lightly rapping on the door, then entered to wish his three-hundred-pound host a hearty "Good morning to you, Captain O'Grady."

The expression on the superintendent's face clearly stated that Ogre wasn't enjoying the sunny day. A large fist slapped his desk.

"You back again?"

"Not a social call, Walter. Merely a brief mission to escort one of your prisoners away, to free you from further responsibility."

"Which'n would that be?"

"Dockery, Broda J."

He handed the pardon to O'Grady's sweating

paw, itching to ask if Miss Tarla would be continuing to pay call, without transportation. Ogre's eyes narrowed, and his lower lip curled to a snarl. "What's the game, Sweetbutter? On purpose you trying to bait me?"

"Not actual."

O'Grady grunted to his feet, returning the document to the chief. "I won't be needing no fancy paper. Your pretty boy Dockery took off. But he won't fly distant."

"Dockery's not *here*?"

"Oh, he'll be here rightful soon. Nobody . . . not in eleven years. Not a nobody ever break out a my jail. But I shall retake him—alive! Bring him back to rot like a drown rat. We'll cold-water hose him at evening, so's he sleep wet and shivery. Eventual, that boy'll pray to die. Beg to. Beg on his knees in the muck."

O'Grady's rage had shortened his breath. Panting like a spent bloodhound, his thick lips were drooling, and almost every word sprayed spittle.

"Allow me to warn you," Percy said. "Dockery is beyond your jurisdiction, sir. Attempting to recapture is a felony. You snatch that fellow, and you'll be arrested for kidnapping. Prosecuted by law." Chief Sweetbutter patted a hip revolver. "Unless *you* stop a bullet while trying to elude me."

He turned to go.

"Hold on," O'Grady told him. "You forgit that Dockery escaped *before* that there *pardon* of yourn got deliver to me. He commit a unlegal act. Therefore, it's my *duty* to retake him." Ogre spat. "And I intend."

Leaving the labor camp, tires scattering gravel, Percival Sweetbutter knew he best do something. Do it sudden. He had to find Dockery before O'Grady found him.

Trouble is, both men knew where to look.

CHAPTER 20

Broda Joe slept.

Not with a ankle linked to a lice-infested prison cot, but in a clean white comfortable double bed. Beside his brother.

During the night, he'd quietly got up to sneak outdoors and throw up Aunt Lulu's delicious eats. As well as some Mexican chow. A shame, yet his stomach couldn't keep hardly anything down. Same way at the labor camp. He mostly lived on water. Almost all of the convicts were thin. So bony they were afraid of falling. Cons who fell on a hard surface usual shattered hip bones, because nobody had flesh to cushion them.

Riding the donkey had made Bro nervous. Had she been a tall horse, the fret of falling would've been terrifying.

Outside, the moon was a dimple on the cheek of night. Sky was blacker than licorice yet softly freckled with grains of stars. The freedom made him thankful—for himself, and for seeing Branch and Tug so solid, behaving as kin ought. Grampap had sort of softened. No longer wintry, his face seemed to thaw warmer, as though he'd discover a new springtime.

Mouselike, Bro crept back to bed, pleased that Tugwell was sleeping, cozy as a curled-up kitten. Bro sighed, relaxed, and again drifted off.

At dawn, he awoke to see Tugwell's sleeping face. "Lord above, please don't allow him to grow up anything like me." He lay quietly, waiting for Tug to stir, realizing he couldn't hide here on the Diamond Dee. Lawmen would be coming. It wouldn't be fair to involve three good people with the family's black sheep.

The ex-con.

Worries of recapture and being returned in chains to the labor camp gave him chills. Before going back, he vowed he'd take his own life. Hang himself. If such happen, who would find his body stretching a rope? It would be tough enough for either Branch or Aunt Lulu. But what if Tugwell found him, hanging dead and cold? He'd have to sneak away. Perhaps now, today, early, to dodge a tearful so long that would break four hearts. Why does living have to hurt so bad? At least he'd brung a donkey for Tugwell.

Last evening, after a corker of a home-cooked meal, he had showed his brother how to mount her broad gray back. How gentle she was. How sweet-natured. It pleased Bro to see Tugwell so confident. They had discussed names for her. None pleased Tug. After each suggestion, he shook his head. Bro gave up, shifting the conversation to how he escaped camp and stole a pink car that belong to Ogre O'Grady's tootsie. He told Tug the lady's name.

"Tarla."

With a wide smile, Tug had nodded to his pet, as though hearing a fitting name for her. Broda Joe had chuckle like to split a gut.

"Tarla? Okay. Tarla she be."

A noise floated up from the kitchen. Aunt Lulu was cranking up cookery. And now Tugwell was awake. Darn! There went Bro's chance to melt into the misty morning and disappear. He hear old Branch taking a pee. Then another sound. One that clenched Broda Joe's fists.

Car engine.

Leaping out of bed, Bro raced across the hall

to a front bedroom window. Below, as the official Yazoo City cruiser stopped, so did his heart.

The law!

A door opened. Out stepped the uniformed chief of police . . . Percival Sweetbutter. Yet he didn't seem to be in a rush. Wasn't wearing a weapon. Tug suddenly joined him at the windowsill, pointing a finger at the chief, nudging Bro and sporting a grin.

"That's right. You and Chief Sweetbutter are ice cream buddies. I forgit. Well, leastwise he ain't prowling after *you*."

Tug no longer smiled.

"Soft now. We don't panic a sweat. I doubt big Percival is come to collar me. Unless . . . unless he got inform about Tarla's machine." Bro squinted. "He's carryin' something blue."

Broda Joe held his breath. His life had always been thisaway. On the edge. He hadn't broke every law on the list, but doggone close. Be wrong to jump too soon? Ha. Better soon than late. Racing back to Tugwell's bedroom, Bro hustled into his clothes. All white. To a mirror he asked, "Who am I fooling?"

Meanwhile, Tug had sneaked downstairs. Bro heard laughing, and Chief Sweetbutter's big booming voice talking about . . . strawberry ice cream? Then his great-aunt chimed in.

"Bless you, Officer."

"You sure made a friend in Tugwell," Branch added. "And us Dockerys owe you grateful, sir."

With a shrug, Bro ventured down the stairs and greeted the group with a hopeful face. In case he'd guessed wrong, also ready to run like a rabbit. Tug had Chief Sweetbutter's official cowboy hat on his head, and grinned happy about it.

"Broda Joe Dockery?" the lawman asked.

Bro answered him. "Guess I'm stuck with being *me*."

The chief tossed a blue-jacketed packet on the parlor table. "Son, this here's a pardon. Honest. It bear the signature of Judge Singletary. Legal and binding. Means you be a free man."

"I'm out?"

The Chief nodded. "You are at liberty. However, let's don't git confident cocky. In my opinion, the ordeal ain't exactly ended."

Chief Sweetbutter calmly reviewed the situation, one that centered not around his office but the Pecan County Correctional Labor Camp and its Boss Man. O'Grady had little to be proud of. Except one fact: Nobody'd ever got away clean.

"I know this man," Percy said. "Ogre's a

thug. The worst kind, a bully behind a badge. He hasn't earned the respect of a single law enforcement officer in the entire State of Florida." He sighed. "He's also a bulldog in pursuit. Once his canine fangs sink into the raw meat of revenge, his jaws lock, and won't let go."

Staring at Bro, he added one more comment. "Son, you're the raw meat."

CHAPTER 21

Ogre had hisself a notion.

As he kicked his office desk, the get-even idea slashed half a sour smile on his mouth, but there be no gladness in it. He'd just do smart and sneak around that cussed *pardon*.

Dockery busted out. He would make Dockery pay. In blood.

Problem be, his deputy wardens was all dumb bunnies. Nary a bit of brain in any of 'em. That's what make his plan so slick, because he'd pit jailbird against jailbird. There wunt be none of his deputies in on the collar.

"I use my meanest cons. Or maybe just one."

He already know which of the convicts had poke sport at the Dockery boy, calling him

Girlie Face. Well, now he'd give them baddies another crack at him. Wouldn't be death. No, it'd be ten time worse. After a while, poor Dockery wouldn't be human no more. Just a cornered crazy animal.

"Dumb."

Ogre knowed he'd done a dumb-ass thing, telling the chief of police that Dockery git away. Simple to see that Percival Sweetbutter work against him. Judge also against him. Weren't fair, both of them peoples on Dockery's side instead of his'n.

Using a con on this caper to nab Dockery, he'd shift the blame on a prisoner, if matters go wrong. Claim he break out.

"Nobody escape Walter P. O'Grady."

Saying so cause another worry to nettle him. Over his shoulder, he admire the award on his office wall. Never got no high school diploma, but at least he have a certificate in a frame, about how he'd be a good warden. For ten year, and going on eleven, nobody escape the Pecan County Correctional Labor Camp. No bird fly.

Until now!

Maybe them county or state bigwigs would be coming to take away his award. Bust up the frame and set fire to his prize.

"Dockery, you little rat. When us'll overtake you, you will be fixing to know how terrible you got *took*."

His hands clenched into hammers.

CHAPTER 22

I watched Aunt Lulu leave. Waving at her.

Taking her Ford to Yazoo City for groceries and to check on her house in Rickapee, she threatened to be back before three men got hungry enough to disaster the kitchen.

Even without her, it was a shiner of a Diamond Dee morning. Grampap took Broda Joe and me to the corral to edify us, so he said, concerning mules. Hefting up Maude's hoof, to cradle gently between his knees like it was delicate crockery, his thumbnail picked out a pebble.

"Mule's hoof grows slower than a horse's. The pores are closer, harder, not so liable to crumble, providing I don't feed 'em to overweight." His hand rubbed her foreleg. "Never see a mule with a splint problem."

"What's splint?" Bro asked.

"I'm no vet. But offhand, I'd guess it's merely a lump of cannon bone. Common in some horses. Not in mules."

Petting Theodore sure was a smooth thing to do. His hair was short, satiny, and he felt warm. Turning his head, Theodore looked me over; deciding I was a friend, he made a soft rumble in his throat.

You talk better than I do.

Hearing Theodore's noise, Branch said, "At times these mules make a lot louder sound than that. A mule can tell you right off if there's anything strange that's prowling around. Especial at night. Don't need a watchdog when mules are standing guard. They'll hee-haw like a burglar alarm."

"Some say they're bright as horses," Bro said.

"Brighter. If I ride Maude in forest, she won't walk under a low tree branch that she can clear but would knock me off. Both our mules are nice-natured. Show me a mean kicky mule, I'll show you a brainless owner."

"Balky?"

Grampap ducked under Theodore and came up yonder. "No. Independent. If this animal don't want to canter, he wunt, and no riding crop'll change his mind. Because there's probable a reason. A owner has to deserve a mule's trust. Fail to do this, and you'll be souring your animal. And yourself."

It pleased me to stroke Tarla. No matter where my hand touched her, she seemed to be touching me.

Grampap's face sudden lit up. "Say," he said, "I just remembered what a neighbor told me about a donkey. Jack Fletcher keeps one for a particular purpose."

Why?

Resting my hand on Grampap's, I let him know that I wanted to hear the reason. And maybe Tarla did, too.

"Jack had trouble with coyotes. Like us. But since he pastured a donkey with his brood cows, the coydogs don't no longer prey on the dropped calfs. Ain't lost a single newborn."

Hearing it made me hug Tarla.

Now listen up to Grampap, I told her. *You can earn your oats around here, even though I don't yet understand how you'll do it.*

I liked it when Grampap was teaching stuff to Broda Joe and me. He weren't no longer heartsore. A changed man, as if a gloomy night had ended and he felt sunlight again. I'd begun to forget what happened all those years ago. Maybe Grampap was also forgetting. Still aplenty of tough bark on him. Yet he seemed to be starting to forgive himself.

Growing up, I didn't feel any closeness to my parents, because they was so icy to each other and to me. And to Bro. When he left for prison camp, it was like our family froze to death. We had to move to Georgia because of the disgrace.

It didn't help. Kids in Georgia didn't take to a Florida boy who couldn't talk. With Bro gone, I had nobody for a friend. But today, here on the ranch, I had Broda Joe again, and Grampap and Aunt Lulu . . . and a good gray donkey. Not to mention Maude and Theodore. In town, Chief Percival Sweetbutter. Perhaps I could earn money and buy us ice cream.

I was a ton better off than before, with my father's smelling of whiskey, or my mother's praying and running to church. To hide.

Another good thing: Last night, Grampap said if I was faithful to my chores and egg collecting, I'd have my own calf to raise. And show at the Pecan County Fair.

Early on, I'd sort of gather that Aunt Lulu didn't recent approve of her brother. That had also changed. Last evening, Branch and Lulu actual did something social together.

They played checkers.

At first, things was peaceable, but when Branch lost three games in a row, his ornery temper heated up. Grampap swatted a few checkers off the board and onto the floor. Without a word, he picked them up and went storming upstairs to bed, his boots kicking the risers. Plain to see that Branch's steamy nature still needed cooling.

Today was a different story. A far better one. Us three men done ranch work for most of the day.

I helped Aunt Lulu fix a nifty supper of cheese on cauliflower, and chicken livers on honey grits. Pickle beets. And cornbread so buttery it was like eating a golden cloud.

Before my brother and I drifted off to sleep, he said something that eased my thinking. "Tugboat, several times today, I seen you almost try to talk. Don't rush it. One the reasons I brung you a donkey is this: When two of you's together, whisper to her. Or hum. If you stutter, or tangle the words, Tarla won't give a gosh all. To her, any soft sound of your voice will be a petting."

Bro, I want someday to talk to you. To say that you really are one heck of a big brother. I'm so proud you're mine.

CHAPTER 23

The telephone jolted me awake.

Ringing, ringing, ringing down in the kitchen until I hear Grampap gripe. "Who in tarnation calls at twenty to five on a Sunday morning?"

Bro stayed asleep, but Aunt Lulu and I hustled downstairs with Branch, curious as cats.

Grampap barked a "Hello" but then listened a spell. "All right," he said serious, "soon's I'm dressed, I'll be to your place. Stay calm, Ramona."

Almost before he hung the receiver on its hook, Aunt Lulu seemed to know who called, and wondered what her trouble was about.

"Ramona Sturgis. Her mare's been down for most the night. Can't expel her foal. Ramona's usual vet, Furman Ebank, don't answer his phone.

Probable out of town. Dang it! I regret telling her I'd go. I can't, Lucretia. And you know the reason."

Clutching the front of her brother's nightshirt, Aunt Lulu snapped at him. "Is there no mustard in you? Branch Dockery, you'd *better* go, as good a neighbor as Ramona's always been. This'll be the remedy to lick your wounds and heal you whole again." Quickly, she looked at me. "And you're to take Tugwell with you."

Grampap's mouth was quivering.

"Lucretia, you know my feeling on horses."

"Indeed I do. Also, how you ought to feel regarding your grandchild. Aloma Ruth is dead. Dead! There's no bringing her back. But this little boy is living. High time to gather up your guts, face it, and stare down the devil that's in you."

As it was slightly cool weather, still dark, Aunt Lulu insist that both Grampap and me wear sweaters. We agreed, then took 'em off in the pickup truck. Branch said, "I don't never argue at her. Usual, I nod, then do whatever I dang well cussed please." His boot stamped the floorboards.

His leathery spirit made me laugh.

Grampap told me, "Mares and foals ain't tough as cattle. A cow'll breach out a calf, rump first, with no bother. But a breached foal can suffocate unless it's yanked quick. In one or two minutes."

Without braking, he turned a corner to bump us along another dirt road that appeared to lead nowhere. Our headlights didn't seem to know either. They seemed to be searching the night.

"The mare's water will break first. Gallons of it'll flood out. You'll see a round bubble. Cloudy white. Then two little hoofs. Nose comes next. Sort of like a diver fixing to dive, extending the tips of both front hoofs under his chin. Heading for light. Soon as the mare's sack breaks open, her baby begins to breathe. We maybe got a foal stuck in a birth canal. Snout's out. But if the tongue is blue, he'll choke. And die. Once oxygen pumps into his lungs, the tongue turns a normal pink, and the foal survives."

Once there, Grampap and I hurried into Miss Ramona's barn, to a stall lit by the yellowy light of three hanging lanterns. A gray-haired woman, sweaty faced, was kneeling in uneven waves of straw. The smell was sickly. A horse lay on her flank, belly swollen, nickering.

"Thank you for coming, Branch. You're a angel."

"Twisted?"

"Afraid so. All I can see at her backside is nostrils and one hoof. Couldn't locate the other."

"Got any grain bags? Full ones?"

She pointed. We moved two fifty-pounders, then rolled the mare over, above them, so her rump was higher than her muzzle. Stripping off his shirt, Grampap was waist-up naked. Hands and face darker than his milky chest.

"Hold her head, Ramona, else she'll hoof me to Kingdom Come." To me, he said, "Tug, I have to retreat her foal. Back, not out, by pushing on the foal's shoulders. Then we can unite a pair of front hoofs."

He pushed, until he couldn't drive the foal in another inch. After smearing his right hand and forearm with the hog lard he'd brung, Grampap tried reaching inside her. Deeper. Several times, straining and grunting, until he was panting.

"Tugwell, she's still twisted. No room for my arm. Yours is thinner. So you'll have to undo her."

No. I can't. We need Bro.

Before I could shake my head, Grampap was peeling off half of my shirt and larding my arm. "Don't ponder about it, boy. Just perform. Probe inside her. . . . Yes! That's right. Deeper. Reach up to your shoulder and find the other foreleg. Pull. Fetch it out."

I don't know how!

The mare's insides were hot and slippery wet. Her rump smelled me to a gag. Frightened, I removed my hand, unable to tell Grampap I couldn't hack it.

"You can do it, Tugwell," he whispered. "You're a Dockery. And you have to because there's nobody else here with a small arm. You're all this suffering mare's got between her and dying! Find the other hoof, grip the leg, and heave it out, and together we'll bring a foal."

Eyes shut, my face almost kissing her wetness, I reached in, felt around. A bone? A leg bone. But as I pulled, not much happen.

"Got it?"

I nodded.

"Take a firm purchase on it. All fingers, like you grip a baseball bat. . . . Good. Now bring it home. Steady. Don't yank. Merely ease it where it natural wants to be."

The mare nickered again, loud, warning me

that I was cramping her insides. When she kicked Branch, he gasped, yet didn't swear. *Somebody help me pull,* how I wanted to holler. But this weren't no time to think about Tugwell Dockery. A more important matter begged doing.

So I took hold, trying not to puke as wet stuff spattered my face. Birthing is awful hot business.

"Good going, boy. We got a pair of little hoofs aligned. From now on, we let the mare birth it herself. Now listen. We only pull when she's resting, to prevent backslide. Retraction. We each hold a hoof so she don't lose progress."

We held, Grampap and I. Ramona slowly worked the mare off of the grain sacks. Now she lay level.

Something very wet stung my eyes so I couldn't see much at first. Only feel. More and more of a very hot thing. Slicker than a eel. Then I saw a face.

Its eyes are open. Grampap, I can see ears. A whole head.

"Shoulders showing. They're the toughest. A foal's widest part, and here they come."

The struggling foal was inside a shred of a gray bag. In tatters. The mare knowed what to do. Curling her muzzle toward us, her teeth tore at the ripped sack and bit at a spiral cord. A part of it whipped like a red snake. Bloody stuff sprayed all over us. Branch's chest and trousers was a soppy mess, and I couldn't seem to either take off my shirt, or put it back on. But I didn't give a doggone.

We done it! Please hear me, Grampap. And we'll both forget about the dead horses. Now we got a living one. A foal.

The mare was up.

On her feet. Her nose was nudging the newborn and demanding it to breathe, and survive. Her tongue licked it. Then licked me with one rough swipe. As the wet foal staggered to his feet on wobbly legs, how I wanted Bro to see it all.

Because of the chilly weather, tiny wisps of mist were rising from the foal's hot body. Unable to stand, the little colt tumbled over and into the straw. His bulging eyes looked confused. Wanting to help, I started to reach for him, until my grandfather warned me off.

"No. Leave him be, Tug. Doing it all hisself will strengthen him with every effort. Just as tackling hard ranch work makes *you* stronger."

Sounded like sense to me.

Even though Grampap and I were sloppy wet, Ramona gave us each a hearty hug. Rattling home in the pickup truck, he was laughing and slapping his knee. "Can't wait to tell Lucretia and Broda Joe what a vet you be. Both'll be right proud of you, Tugwell. Ya done noble."

Smiling, I plumb forgot how smelly I stunk. Not a bit dirty. About as clean as God could make me.

CHAPTER 24

A bright Sunday morning.

Uncomfortable for Percival Sweetbutter to pry open his bloodshot eyes. Even his hair hurt. “Never again.” He’d made that promise before.

Perched on the edge of his sagging bed, he regretted not leaving the Saturday night poker game earlier to go home and dent a pillow. In the bathroom, he worked up the courage to confront a mirror. His unshaved face looked like hammered garbage. Over a steamy mug of black coffee, Percy decided against attending church. His hands were too unsteady to hold a hymnal. Instead of formal devotions, he’d do a good deed for the Dockerys.

A preventative measure.

He recollected a road, mostly ruts and soft earth, that run from O'Grady's labor camp toward the Dockerys' Diamond Dee cattle ranch. A back way. It meandered through miles of wild swamp.

This would be his morning chore.

By early afternoon, if he felt a bit more in fettle, he'd attend the baseball game. To root for the Yazoo Zooters.

Forcing himself into comfortable clothes, not his uniform just yet, Percy groaned into the car and started on his mission. He located the deserted road. No fresh tire tracks. Good. Seesawing the steering wheel several spins until the car was perpendicular to the red clay road, he cross marked it, sideways. At right angles to the ruts. Later, he'd be able to tell whether or not a vehicle passed this way, headed for the Dockery property.

"Now then," he said aloud, "if'n I was Captain Walter O'Grady, and I suspect a runaway named Dockery might seek haven at the Diamond Dee cattle enterprise, which route do I take to attack the place? The very one I cross tired with my patrol car." He made a mental note to check this back route as often as possible. And pass the word to a deputy.

CHAPTER 25

Upon returning from Ramona's, Grampap and I were yawning for a breakfast. No dice, as Lucretia Louise Dockery had other plans. When all four of us were soaped, scrubbed, and into clean duds, we boarded her Model T. Branch in front. Broda Joe and I in back.

"Well, where to?" Grampap growled as she started the car.

"It's nigh to Sunday noon. How shameful that I've neglected the Sabbath devotions of this family."

"Don't make sense to go hungry," Branch grumbled.

"Does to me. Instead of our bellies and bowels," Aunt Lulu said, "we righteous ought to nourish our souls."

"Why today?"

"Because something precious good happened early this morning in Ramona's barn. In addition, Bro is home. Now that the Dockerys be final collected, best we bow thanks."

When she made a certain turn, Branch said, "How well I recall, Lucretia, when you and I were kidsters, we'd ride up here bareback and barefoot on a old strawberry roan."

Aunt Lulu said, "His name was Clarence."

Broda Joe kept quiet, content to gaze out a car window. And I was too tuckered out to do much more'n coast.

"You boys," Aunt Lulu said, "are in for a sumptuous surprise."

We chugged along through the lonely stillness of a pine thicket. Tree trunks straighter than soldiers, a wooden army that can only stand at attention but cannot march. Once up a gentle rising that overlook a river, Aunt Lulu stopped the engine. Climbing out of the Ford, I heard singing from below. The voices shined like new pennies. On two blankets, we sat in oak shade, to view a entire congregation of colored folks. Men in black. The ladies in white, some holding umbrellas to hide from the heat.

"It's a all-day conversion," Bro whispered.

"The fellow in the white robe, up to his waist in water . . . he the preacher. The three men and two ladies, with white cloth on their heads, are to be baptized."

"Proper so," said Aunt Lulu. "A true baptism isn't a sprinkle. It's a full dunking in living water. That means water that is not contained, but flowing free. To the sea."

"As a boy," Branch said, "I swum naked in that there deep spring. Water's colder than a well-digger's butt."

"Watch your mouth," Aunt Lulu warned him.

Hearing the singing, sort of a soft hum, turned both Broda Joe and me to serious. Bro's eyes closed as if breathing in a steady hymn that didn't quit. There didn't seem to be any words to it, yet the music began to fill me. Better than breakfast.

Grampap wasn't as convinced. "Makes me wonder," he snorted, "about all these holy conversions. Do they last?"

"Perhaps not." Aunt Lulu shot him a forgiving look. "A bath doesn't last either. But once in a spell we all could use one."

To me, that's what our Sunday together had become. A musical bath. My foot couldn't help tapping to the tune. Not rapid. The rhythm was unhurried, like the river.

"Them people," Bro said, "are the bugles of Jehovah."

On the hillside above the river, we stayed for most a hour. I didn't want to leave. As the people were singing, I sang, too. Inside. Blooming in my head like a rainbow of flowers. Music I could smell and taste.

"Lucretia Louise," Grampap said as we started for home, "you proved right. Thanks for carrying us there, Sister. I am truly grateful."

Aunt Lulu said, "Gratefulness is the highest note in the hymn of prayer."

CHAPTER 26

A sleepy Sunday afternoon.

At last we had eaten. Four full stomachs helped to quiet most everyone into peaceful. Shoes off, Aunt Lulu was napping on the parlor sofa. Grampap doing a likewise in one of the front porch chairs.

Broda Joe was on edge. "Tugboat, let's go visit your donkey."

His suggestion was a excuse, to crack a tough nut to his brother. Soon, a lot sooner than later, Bro felt he'd best leave the Diamond Dee to locate a paying job, if he could muster up the muscle to hold one down. No way could he sponge off elderly kin. Ought to get away from Yazoo City, where half the town viewed him as nothing but a jailbird.

He'd try not to stray too far.

"Tarla, there you be. Ears up."

With no coaxing, the donkey came to greet them.

"Sometime, when you and Tarla work together, like a team, you'll be saying stuff to her just the way you always do with me. And then your words'll git spoke in a whisper." Looking at Tug, he could tell the boy was already conversating with his donkey.

Turning away, Bro coughed hard. There was a poison in his lungs that refused to hack out. He figured how the cough started. O'Grady had rent out workers to a nearby pulp mill. Cheap labor. None of the cons saw a cent of the money. For several months, Broda Joe unloaded clay and soda ash from railroad cars. The toxic white powders were not contained in bags, and the dust from the scoop machine peppered every breath a man took.

His lungs were getting worse, more hurtful, and he frequent hacked up red specks. By law, there'd been a so-called doctor who checked the convicts every six weeks. His fingernails was always dirty and his breath reeked of liquor. He reminded Bro of his father. When there was something serious wrong, Doc Stanton operated. Slash with a knife, the prisoners said. That was the reason Bro never complained to him. With luck, his chest might heal. The outdoor ranch air was a pleasure to breathe. So there was a chance his overall health could improve.

Tug noticed his coughing, stared at him, then looked uphill to the cemetery. His eyes seemed to be asking a question: *Bro, are you fixing to die?*

"Everbody dies, Tug. Trees, flowers, fish, snakes, birds, animals . . . and people. Seeing as I'm eighteen, nine years older than you be, I'll go before you will. Cons die young."

Tug shook his head.

"When I go, dig me a narrow grave, on account there's little but lean on my bones. Been too busy to fetch fat. Y'all won't have much of me to bury."

Hurts so much to spit out honest, Bro thought, yet it was his duty. To tell it straight. No lies, not between brothers. To avoid crying, he helped Tug up and onto Tarla's back. No words necessary. Bro hoped that Tug didn't start thinking that spoken words mean brains. Some stupes do nothing but shoot off a mouth. No sense pours out. They're just firing a empty popgun.

"That's right. Rub her backbone free of itching."

Bro had to look away, far across the Florida outback flats, with a horizon line broken by the tall procession of sabal palm. Our past is here, he thought, and still singing its own song. The Diamond Dee. Although he'd never been a part of it, Broda Joe somehow felt anchored in this Dockery land.

Tugwell Dockery's land.

Tug didn't yet realize that someday he'd inherit every square inch, every square mile. With a hefty helping of luck, Lucretia Louise and Branch be sturdy enough to survive a few more years, even a decade.

"Our Diamond Dee," Bro said without thinking.

Hearing him, Tug slid off Tarla, dropped a knee to the sandy soil, and with a fingertip, drawed the family's cattle brand:

CHAPTER 27

He play it real sly.

The truck rolled through the night. To his left, behind the steering wheel, the dumb cluck's wrists be cuffed. Chained just loose enough to steer and gear. Ankles hobble by fourteen inch of chain, able to step on a clutch or gas pedal. But shackled, to prevent a nimble get-away.

Dressed in black-and-white zebra stripes, his patsy jailbird was restrained in iron, above and below.

Keys stay at the office. Hid.

O'Grady pat hisself on the back because he ordered the prisoner to drive. Savvy move. Had he sat hisself to steer the camp's junk-heap vehicle, his right-hip .38 revolver would be riding betwixt them, in view and in reach. Only a inch or two from Crit Zaggert's untrusty paw.

Too easy a grab.

While shifting, Zaggert give Ogre a sneaky glance. Like a coiled snake. This no-good con already plan a double-cross, though nary a word git spoke outa Crit's stubble face. Mum as dynamite before it explodes. The other inmates call him The Critter. Inside, Crit be top dog at the labor camp. The head con weren't too famous for humanitary ways. He act meaner than a tail-up scorpion.

Crit's eyes was so cold, they'd bite.

In spite of the fact that he was near double Zaggert's size, O'Grady was wary of this man. The Critter weren't black or high yella or pale convict white. Crit be the color of mud, like he crawl out of swamp muck.

Zaggert be a lifer. No parole for a homicide conviction.

As the clunker of a camp truck bounce in and out of potholes, O'Grady reviewed his plan. At the Dockery place, he'd hold the gun, allowing Crit to do the talking. Make a threat. Walter O'Grady had smarts. First off, to pull a caper on a Sunday night. Cops all tired out from Saturday hoopla. In case the Dockery brat git killt, instead of took alive, he'd arrange for Crit Zaggert to take full blame.

A warden's word against a con's.

O'Grady squint, and then point.

"Turn right, here."

Without reducing speed, Zaggert wrench the steering wheel, to scrape against a thicket of kudzu vine and tall butterfly weed. Hook-thorn palmetto lashed the windshield like a bad temper.

"Hey! Take it slow, ya lead foot. You probable done all that a purpose, and don't tell me no different."

The truck slowed. For certain, few vehicles used this excuse for a road. Winding and bumpy. No traffic, which suited O'Grady, as tonight's romp weren't what the authorities would call legal. But necessary. Had to maintain his perfect record of eleven years. More important, to git even with Dockery for escaping.

"Stop!"

Crit Zaggert's sudden stomp on the brake caused O'Grady's hat to fall off. No matter. They'd come to a clearing.

"Leave it run neutral." O'Grady point a thick finger. "There be cattle over yonder, close by that fence. Go check if they's got a Diamond Dee brand." Drawing his pistol, Ogre smirk.

"And best you dassn't try to slither out of sight."

Zaggert done as told, then shuffle his chainy feet back to the truck. Nodding, he use a fingertip to trace a ◇ and a ▷ on the dusty windshield.

"This'n here the target. So turn off them headlights, shift her into low gear, and ease her forward. Remember, like I warn you at camp, we ain't after nobody but Girlie Face. Snatch and skip."

He reholster his weapon. But kept his hand around the butt.

No expression on Crit Zaggert's face. A blank, like he don't hear, feel, or care about living. Maybe he already dead. A ghost? The thought give Walter O'Grady a chill. His hand lifted to protect his neck.

Passing under a arch with a ◇▷ overhead, he command Zaggert to slow to a crawl. Soon as some small yellow lights pinpoint the distance, maybe a mile away, O'Grady grab the ignition keys. Engine died. He figure the time be perfect. About eight o'clock, or past. They'd wait patient. Ranchers sack out early as chickens. O'Grady lit up a Camel and smoked it. Then a second, but didn't bother to offer even a butt to his prize prisoner. He just blow a few drags at him. Crit's serpent eyes never flinch.

Getting out, they walk toward the place where, one by each, the lights go out. Dockerys soon asleep. Would there be dogs? Ugly watchers that run loose? This danger he hadn't figure on and it make him sweat. However, the idea of revenge was so tasty that a dog wouldn't stand in his way. Nothing would.

Under his breath, he said, "Ain't a nobody gonna make a jackass out of Captain Walter P. O'Grady."

He hadn't count on mules.

At first, the braying was sort of a once or twice, but then their honking begin to saw into the night's darksome. O'Grady swore. Well, if'n he had to shoot a stupid mule, he would, to git what he'd sneak here for. A dead Dockery mule weren't no tragedy.

Not much progress in nearing the house. Ogre was three hundred pound of lazy lard, and tiring. His prisoner's ankle shackles only permitted a awkward shuffle of inches. Hardly a stride. Holding up wrists, Crit plead to have the warden unlock and remove his upper and lower cuffs.

O'Grady shook his head. "Not a chance. And the keys is back at camp. Just in case. So don't try no fancy notions."

He spoke too loud and the mules agreed, persisting their hee-haw snorts until O'Grady was fixing to lose temper. "We still be a quarter mile from the house. So how come those cussed mules know we's out here in the gloom?"

No answer from Zaggert. But a house light flicked on. Then another, a bright porch lantern that lit up two vehicles—a pickup truck and a black car. Look to be a Ford.

"Hey! Best we git back to our machine first, and maybe ram into them two cars, so's peoples can't foller us."

They retreated. Reaching his truck, leaning on a front fender, O'Grady was short of breath, mouth open, puffing and panting harder than his heart could pump. His weight was a load to lug. Made him angry to notice that Zaggert wunt winded. He wanted to fall down and pass out. If he did, Ogre knowed how long he'd survive with this cottonmouth con.

About one second.

CHAPTER 28

The mules woke him.

Choking on fear, having a horrible dream about being brutalized at the labor camp, Broda Joe broke a sudden sweat. Had to be a reason Maude and Theodore bray so loud. Again, and again, hacksawing the night.

Tug's eyes popped open. Asking.

"Maybe it's coyotes. You sleep," Bro told him.

A crash of metal on metal, as though a traffic accident happen. Out front. Dashing across the upstairs hall, Bro peered through a open window. A heavy truck had piled into Grampap's pickup and Aunt Lulu's Ford. With the aid of a porch light, he read the letters on the familiar truck's open door.

Fighting a fit of coughing that watered his eyes, he knew Chief Sweetbutter had guess right. He'd predict that O'Grady might seek revenge, come here, and try to retake him. But when a man in stripes dismounted the truck, it weren't Ogre.

It was Zaggert. The Critter.

Cuffed hands held a raised bullhorn. A voice spoke. Spooky. Like the hiss of a snake. "Girlie Face, you in there? Show yourself. Come out with both hands on top a yo pretty head. You hear me?"

Aunt Lulu gasped.

Branch did a plenty more.

Broda Joe heard a sharp *click clack* as Grampap lever a cartridge into the firing chamber of his aging Winchester. Glancing to his right, Bro saw its steely muzzle poke forward, out an upstairs window. Without delay, the rifle fired. The camp truck's windshield shattered. Inside it, somebody in the passenger seat cussed and shot a pistol. Twice.

"Branch!" Aunt Lulu screamed.

Grampap moaned as he lost control of the

Winchester. The rifle fell, clattering down the rough shingles of the slanted porch roof, to smack the stony walkway.

Seeing it, Zaggert started forward. But he was thirty feet distant and both his ankles were hobbled by a short chain. Broda Joe didn't pause to think. Diving out of the window, he rolled down the roof's steep incline, and fell onto the stones. His shoulder hit with a *thud*. He felt a bone break. More than one, and the cracking pains pierced into him, deeper than daggers.

Hurt to breathe. And he tasted blood.

Crawling to the rifle, he noticed its trigger housing had worked loose. The Winchester was broken and couldn't fire. Nonetheless, Bro forced himself to crouch, almost stand, and point the rifle at Crit Zaggert. He wouldn't git took alive.

Broda Joe Dockery wasn't returning to Hell.

He choose Heaven.

Directing the broken rifle at the advancing Zaggert, he worked the lever, pretending he'd load a second cartridge. Raising it to his shoulder hurt dreadful, yet he sighted at The Critter. His finger curved around a busted trigger.

Nobody would know.

Broda Joe saw O'Grady's pig face leaning

out of the truck's passenger window, leveling a revolver at his chest. "Drop it, boy. I'm a-taking you back."

Bro had only a blink of time. Branch was wounded. If there was another gun anywhere in the house, Aunt Lulu might know about it, fetch it, start shooting and get herself killt. Along with Tug. Bro switched the rifle's aim from Zaggert to O'Grady. Smiling, he tugged a useless trigger.

"You taking me nowhere. I'm dying free."

CHAPTER 29

Sunday wasn't a day of rest.

Not for a chief of police. At the baseball game, the Yazoo Zooters were losing by three runs. Bottom of the ninth. Some local fans got a mite upset with the plate umpire, Frank Foy, and his controversial view of the strike zone. Suggestions got hooted regarding Frank's ancestry, eyesight, and need for glasses. Pop bottles were launched.

Percy had to cool a few temperatures. In custody.

However, the afternoon did afford a pleasanter moment. Chief Sweetbutter was about to deflower another hot dog, his fifth, when Judge Hannah T. Singletary hailed him at the refreshment stand. They agreed that the game's outcome, with two out, didn't look too rosy for the Zoots.

The Judge said, "Yesterday, instead of bass fishing, I paid an inspection visit to an establishment I've neglected for several years . . . our disgraceful Pecan County Correctional Labor Camp."

Percy became interested. "And?"

Following a swig of root beer, His Honor continued. "Tomorrow morning, I'll telephone Tallahassee and report that disgrace. Chief, we are going to *correct* that sewer. And I mean close it down."

"For keeps?"

The Judge nodded.

Sunday evening was a blessing. Home at last, Chief Percival Sweetbutter removed his boots and skinned off his stockings. Feet up, veined ankles crossed, he settled into a overstuff chair and clicked on the radio. Rudy Vallee, one of his favorite crooners, was singing something real sporty about dear old Maine. His next number was more to Percy's taste, slow and easygoing. Rudy could warble "Beautiful Dreamer" like he'd writ the ballad just for exhausted law enforcement officers.

Even before the songster trilled his final note, Percy's eyes had gently closed.

Strange . . . his parlor clock was striking. Ten bongs.

"Doggone." He'd forget to do a look-see at the road he cross marked, the back route near the Dockerys' ranch. Jumping up, he stumbled, wincing at the needles in a foot that had also fallen asleep. A bare toe stubbed a chair leg. After strapping on his weapon belt, Percy ignored socks, but grabbed his boots. In less than a minute he was pushing the Yazoo City patroller to the maximum. Pitch dark out. He fought a urge to crank up the siren. Why wake up voters?

After all, it was a quiet and peaceful Sunday night, a hour when not a usual lot happen. Leastwise, not in Yazoo.

But something had! Reaching the entrance to the narrow dirt road, the car's searchlight lit up where his tires had crossed the earth. Sure enough, a heavy vehicle had passed over them. Recently, and in a hurry.

Sand was sprayed.

After six miles of furious driving, Chief Sweetbutter saw the accident. P. C. C. L. C. truck had crashed headlong into a cypress trunk.

The driver's door was open, hanging by a single hinge. Gun drawn, suspecting the truck wasn't empty, he approached it with caution.

The hood felt hot.

A sharp odor of gasoline.

His left hand worked a flashlight to encircle the cab's interior. No movement. Percy tucked away his revolver. Only one extra-large occupant, but he hadn't been driving. The vacated driver's seat indicated a hint of warmth. After the impact, the other guy must've vanish into the blackness of night. No footprints. Not a trace. Percy's light beam swept the thick jungle wall of uninviting greenery. KEEP OUT, it seemed to warn. "In that swamp, ample with gators and water mocs, the poor devil won't stand a chance. He'll not even see morning."

Keys dangle from the ignition.

An exposed wrist felt slightly warm yet produced no pulse. No visible weapon. Neither blood nor wounds. A leather hip holster lay empty, its pocket yawning open as if hollering for help. Perhaps due to the smashup, the passenger's fleshy face had been severely twisted to one side. There were purple bruises on his throat.

Something, or *someone*, had broken his neck. No doubt from behind. Wearing handcuffs?

Percy crouched, shining his torch at the face.

His suspicion was verified.

O'Grady.

No sign of a driver. Whoever he was, the fool run into the swamp and to a certain death. Unless. . . . the labor camp truck had obvious been retreating from the northerly direction of the Dockery cattle ranch. So best he hustle over there to check if everybody in one piece. Percy prayed so.

He'd come to like those folks.

CHAPTER 30

I stayed behind.

The six others left our little square cemetery on the knoll to walk slowly and sadly toward the house. Nobody spoke. Even the mockingbirds were still.

Grampap's chest and shoulder had been bandaged for three days, since the shooting. Doctor Munson had extracted the bullets. Two slugs. Doc said that my grandfather was a true Dockery. He added that cattle ranchers like Branch and Lucretia Louise just had to wear out. Like a pair of work boots.

Aunt Lulu guided Branch along, knowing how hard he'd been tooling on the wood for two days, sawing, sanding, and carefully carving the letters. In spite of his gunshot wounds.

Earlier, she'd prepared orange muffins, sponge cake, and lemonade, to offer to anyone attending the funeral.

Four people came.

Chief Sweetbutter. Farley Hill, a young deputy. Mr. Gilbarton, who owned Gil's Garage in town. On Monday, he'd brung the wrecker to haul and repair Aunt Lulu's car and Grampap's pickup. Miss Drinkwine, a retired schoolteacher who been fond of my brother in grade six. "My," she said to Aunt Lulu, "how that child could read. And smack a baseball. Always hoped that Broda Joe would play on our Zooters."

I didn't want any food.

Standing alone, beneath a pecan tree and a oak, studying a low mound of fresh dirt, I only wanted to be with my brother. Aunt Lulu claimed that Bro went to Heaven. All I knowed was a undertaker and a coroner come to gather up his cold stiff body.

Yesterday, they return him to us inside a black hearse. Nailed in the darkness of a plain plank box. Out of sight.

With nobody else's help, I'd dug my brother's grave. Not hard to do in soft Florida sand. Our cemetery plot now had four graves. The trio of older ones had wooden markers, three foot tall, curved at the top and gray from weathering. Grampap had added a fourth, also handmade, but it wasn't yet gray. Bro's marker looked light and fresh and young. When I pressed my face against it, the wood smelled clean. Pure. Like anise leaves.

During the short service, my grandfather read a psalm from our family Bible, and everyone said something good about Bro. Except me.

Before learning me how, my brother read me stories and poems about where mermaids sing, a skylark, and a boy on a burning deck. We went around the world with our brave hero, Mr. Richard Halliburton, and rafted on the Mississippi River with Huck and Nigger Jim. Then to England; for Mole, Ratty, Badger, Mr. Toad . . . and Ivanhoe.

To joyless Mudville, where mighty Casey struck out.

Bro had me printing letters into words, telling me that someday my wording could hatch into stories. Adventures about us.

"Here in Yazoo City," Bro told me, "a plenty of kids ain't readers. Sure, there's a library, where they can read for *free*. But a half of 'em won't." He poked me with a finger. "But if you and me crack open good books, we'll go by them gum chewers like they was parked with the brake on."

His funeral was probable the smallest that Yazoo ever had. Surely the leanest coffin. As Bro said, in a narrow grave. So little of him to bury.

Yet so much to miss.

Here lay Broda Joe Dockery, age eighteen . . . troublemaker, stone thrower and window breaker, a school dropout, likker transporter, labor camp convict and car thief. That's possible what Yazoo thought of him. Reading of his death in the weekly newspaper or police records, they can whisper: "One less punk."

I pity them. Few citizens in Yazoo City, Florida, ever knowed the boy he really was. Or the stand-tall man he might have become.

Kneeling, I rested the palm of my hand on the gritty soil that covered him, wishing that God had taken me, and spared my brother. *Bro, you're not under the ground. You're above the sky. Beyond the white clouds, where there is no labor camp. No coughing or broken bones. Or fear. But you'll still hear Tugboat.*

To honor him, and all of my family, I'd made a few promises. To work honest at my chores, and also look for what needs doing. Branch and Aunt Lulu were taking care of me now. But in a few years I'd be tending to them, and willingly. I promise to speak aloud to Tarla, my donkey. A word at a time. Eventual, bragging about Broda Joe Dockery. Reread the books we shared and a lot more. I will go to school. Here at home, learn how to ramrod a cattle ranch called the Diamond Dee. Maybe even own a horse. Best of all, talk friendly to everyone I'd meet.

Standing, eyes closed, I saw him again. At the end, Broda Joe was about as used up and wore out as that old baseball glove he wanted me to keep. Along with our unspoken secrets only a brotherhood can know.

Trying so hard, and in so many ways to give me a life, Bro gave me his.